The Master Criminal by Fred M White

Fred Merrick White was born in 1859 in West Bromwich in the Midlands of England to Joseph White and Helen Merrick who had married the previous year.

Joseph was a solicitor's managing clerk, who by the time the family moved to Hereford a few years later, had become a solicitor's article clerk.

Little is known of White's early years but what is known is that he followed in his father's footsteps and worked as a solicitor's clerk in Hereford. His father by now had also become a solicitor and times seemed quite prosperous for the family.

However in the late 1880's something went badly wrong for his father and he was imprisoned.

White had by now decided that writing was a more preferable career for him than the law. By 1891 Fred M. White, now 31 years old, was working full-time as a journalist and author, earning enough to support himself and his mother, Helen. By this time Fred's younger brother, Joseph A. White, had left home and working as a glass-blower.

In 1892, White married Clara Jane Smith. The wedding took place at King's Norton, Worcestershire, and the couple went on to have two children; Sydney Eric White (1893) and Ormond John White (1895).

As the century closed Fred's father had been released from prison and was living as a "retired solicitor", together with Helen, in Worthington in West Sussex.

By the time of the 1911 census, Fred M. White, now 52 years old, and his wife Clara were living at Uckfield, a town in the Wealden district of East Sussex. As the ominous shadows of the First World War gathered White had established himself as a popular and extremely prolific author. Indeed whether it was novels or short stories they flowed from his pen with a startling speed and many of them were initially serialized in the popular weekly and monthly magazines. His clever use of science to create imaginative and highly adventurous story lines was a particular talent of his.

During the First World War, both of his sons served as junior officers in The Royal Inniskilling Fusiliers.

The titanic struggle of the First World War and his sons' war-time experiences in it greatly influenced this phase of his writing. His novel The Seed of Empire (1916), describes early trench warfare in great and gritty detail. He went on to describe how the social changes after the war created many problems for returning soldiers as they attempted to fit back into a now peaceful society.

Fred and Clara spent their twilight years in Barnstaple in Devon, an area which also provided the backdrop for his novels The Mystery Of Crocksands, The Riddle Of The Rail, and The Shadow Of The Dead Hand.

Fred Merrick White died in Barnstaple in 1935.

Index of Contents

THE HEAD OF THE CAESARS

CHAPTER I

The history of famous detectives, imaginary and otherwise, has frequently been written, but the history of a famous criminal—never.

This is a bold statement, but a true one all the same. The most notorious of rascals know that sooner or later they will be found out, and therefore they plan their lives accordingly. But they are always found out in the end. And yet there must be many colossal rascals who have lived and died apparently in the odour of sanctity. Such a character would be quite new to fiction, and herein I propose to attempt the history of the Sherlock Holmes of malefactors.

Given a rascal with the intellect of the famous creation in question, and detection would be reduced to a vanishing point. It is the intention of the writer to set down here some of the wonderful adventures that befell Felix Gryde in the course of his remarkable career.

Every schoolboy knows the history of the rise and progress of the Kingdom of Lystria. Forty years ago a clutch of small independent states in South-Eastern Europe, the lapse of less than half a century had produced one of the most powerful combinations on the face of the universe. As everybody also knows, this result was produced by the genius of a quartette who in their time made more history than falls to the lot of the most stormy century. For years they kept the makers of atlases busy keeping pace with the virile growth of Lystria.

But time brings everything in due course; the aged makers of Empire laid aside the pen and the sword, and death came at length to the greatest of the four, even unto Rudolph Caesar, whom men called Emperor of Lystria. Wires, red-hot with the burden of the message, flashed the news to the four corners of the earth; column after column of glowing obituary were thrown together by perspiring "comps"; Caesar's virtues were trumpeted far and wide. It was the last sensation he was like to make.

Meanwhile Mantua, the capital of Lystria, had arranged for a month of extravagant funeral pomp and circumstance fitting the occasion. The papers teemed with the sombre details. The laying in state—a matter of eight days— was to be a kind of glorified Lyceum stage effect. The cold Caesarian clay was to be given over to no vile earthworm, but had been embalmed without delay.

All this pageant Felix Gryde had read of in the seclusion of his London lodgings, in Barton Street. The florid extravagance of the Telegraph awoke in him a vein of poetic heroism—daring with something Homeric in it. The slight, quiet-looking man with the pale features and mild blue eyes did not look unlike the popular conception of a minor poet, save for the fact that Gryde was clean of garb and kept his hair cut.

A smile trembled about the corners of his sensitive mouth.

"Here is a chance," he murmured, "for a really clever soldier of fortune like myself to distinguish himself. I can see in this the elements of the most remarkable and daring crime in the history of matters predatory. Here is a handful of glorified dust guarded night and day by the flower of an army. The stage is brilliantly lighted, passionate pilgrims are constantly coming and going. What a thing it would be to steal that body and hold it up to the ransom of a nation."

Gryde sat thinking this over until the roar of London's traffic sank to a sulky whisper. He might have been asleep, dead, in his chair. Then he rose briskly, lighted a cigarette, and turned up the lamp again. He rang the bell, and a servant entered. The man waited for his master's orders.

"Lye," said Gryde, "I am going away for a day or two. You will get everything ready for me to leave Charing Cross by the nine train in the morning. You will get a letter from Paris saying when I shall return."

The man bowed silently and went out. Then Gryde retired to bed and slept like a child till the morning. Before nightfall he found himself speeding along in a certain continental express towards his destination. Through the blackness of the next night, looking out of the window of the carriage, he could see a faint saffron arc of flame beating down from the sky, the reflection of the countless points of fire in the city of mourning. Gryde's destination was reached, for Mantua was at hand. The train drew into the station.

"One against half a million," Gryde muttered: "a pin's point to a square of bayonets. A good thing I speak the language perfectly."

He took up his handbag, and plunged unheeded into the heart of the city.

CHAPTER II

Nothing more sombre and at the hangings same time more magnificent in the way of a spectacle had ever been witnessed than the ceremonial daily taking place in the chancel of the cathedral at Mantua.

Every window in that immense structure had been darkened by crape the Corinthian columns were draped in the trappings of woe, dark cerements which only served to show up the genius of carver and architect.

The cathedral was faintly illuminated by thousands of candles. The body of the dead monarch lay upon a bare wood bier which made a vivid contrast to the velvet trappings, the piled-up pyramids of flowers, and the brilliant uniforms of the surrounding guards.

These latter, men picked for their fine physique, stood almost motionless around the bier. All down the nave a double line of them were drawn up, and every faithful subject had to pass between them on the way to pay a last tribute of respect to the dead monarch.

They came literally in their thousands, quiet, subdued, and tearful. It was easy for a stranger to mingle with the throng and notice everything: there were dusky corners and quaint, deep oaken stalls where those who cared could hide and watch the progress of the pageant.

Two men had crept behind the gorgeous line of guards into one of these. They had no fear of being detected, lost as they were in the gloom. An additional security was lent by the nebulous wreath of smoke rising from thousands of candles. The features of one of the men were pale, his build as slight; he had deep blue eyes and a sensitive mouth. As to his companion, it matters very little. He was merely the confederate necessary to the carrying out of Gryde's scheme. Gryde did not require his tools to think: that part of the business he always looked to himself. All he wanted was one to faithfully carry out his instructions, to act swiftly, and to possess indomitable courage. There was not a town in Europe where Gryde could not lay his hand upon a score such. For the rest this man passed under the name of Paul Fort.

"A devil of an undertaking," muttered the latter.

"Nothing of the kind," Gryde replied: "the thing is absurdly simple. I admit that on the face of it the stealing of an Emperor from under the eyes of his people is a difficult matter. You shall see. The easiest conjuring tricks always seem the most astounding. From our point of view, £100,000 lies waiting on those bare boards for us. Some people may call those the ashes of departed Caesar—they represent a carcase which, will prove a valuable market commodity."

"But you must get your carcase first."

"I am going to. How? By a conjuring trick. I shall spirit the departed Caesar right from under the eyes of his afflicted people. When? This very evening when the crowd will be at its thickest. Do you see that grating right behind the bier? Well, that communicates with the vaults. The custodian of the vaults will sleep very soundly when he retires this evening, and he will temporarily lose possession of his keys. Not that he will be any wiser for that. It was very thoughtful indeed for the architect who built this place to prepare and execute so minute a plan of the building. I have been studying it very carefully in the library here. This grating now supplies the chancel with hot air. You have already gathered that this evening I shall have the keys of the vaults. Now you hear what to do. Be good enough to repeat your instructions."

"I am to come here alone," Fort said, "about ten o'clock. Then I am to make my way up into the gallery, the key of which you have given me, and I am to remain out of sight till you give a certain signal. Then one by one, at intervals of half a minute, I am to drop those big glass marbles you gave me into the chancel and amongst the congregation. Then I am to leave by the leads, climb down the lightning-conductor at the end of the Chapel of Our Lady, and join you at our lodgings without delay."

"Good," Gryde muttered. "There is no more to be said. Go."

It was the sixth evening of the lying in state and the popular holiday in Mantua. The great cathedral was absolutely packed with people. So great was the crush that the police responsible for order looked grave and anxious. Still the occasion was one of gloom and seemliness, and the procession moved slowly. Even up to the bier the crowd was so thick that only here and there were the scarlet and gold uniforms of the guards picked out vividly against the dense black.

Over the tread of restless feet and the sound of smothered mourning rose the wail of the organ chanting dirges for the departed. The candles guttered and smoked, as the waves of hot air drifted over them. The very solemnity of the place carried awe into the hearts of the spectators. The sudden bang and jar of a falling chair came with a startling echo.

A second later and a glittering globe came swiftly towards the floor. It might have been one of the golden points of the great corona there. It came speeding down like an arrow from a bow, and then suddenly faded into nothingness.

As it did so a hurricane blast seemed to fill the cathedral, a tremendous explosion followed, the vast audience reeled and rocked as if from the shock of a cavalry charge. Ere they could recover from the surprise, another explosion followed.

The piping scream from a woman's throat rang into the roof. With one accord the audience turned a sea of grey faces towards the big west doors. It only wanted the pressure of a child's hand now to set the avalanche in motion. Another and a louder roar followed, there came a roaring wind, the countless candles flared and hissed, and then came the new horror of darkness.

"For Heaven's sake, the doors!" rang out a voice familiar enough to every soldier in Mantua. "Don't rush there; the danger cannot be so very great."

The stern command seemed to hold, the human sheep. As the doors rolled back, the points of flame from the street lamps twinkled through the opening. The black wave rolled steadily on, and a fearful disaster was averted. In a few moments, save for the guard, the cathedral was deserted. Meanwhile the explosions appeared to have ceased. The guard struggled up to the chancel, and after a time the candles were lighted again. Strange to say, not a single human form lay on the marble floor.

"What could it have been?" muttered an officer.

"Nihilists," replied the colonel of the guard. "A foolish display, and intended for show alone. Still, the disaster might have been a terrible one."

The young lieutenant said nothing. His limp hand fell from the waxed point of his moustache, his eyes were fixed upon the bier. The colonel had seen fright before, and, being a brave man, respected it.

"What is the matter?" he asked. The lieutenant found his voice at last.,

"Look there," he said in a frozen whisper. "The Emperor! The scoundrels have been successful. The bier is empty. Why do such wretches live?"

An oath crept from under the colonel's grizzled beard. The shaking of his hand alone betrayed the emotion that he felt.

"My God!" he murmured. "I had died rather than this had happened."

CHAPTER III

It would be idle to attempt to describe the sensation created by the disappearance of the late Emperor of Lystria. Europe had not been so thrilled since the assassination of a one time Czar of Russia. The daily papers teemed with the latest news, and rumours current as to the reasons for the outrage.

Naturally the plot was laid at the door of the Nihilists, and countless arrests were made. But search high and low as they could, no trace of the body could be found. In vain a free pardon was offered to anyone connected with the crime who would come forward and make confession, in vain was a large reward offered.

Count Desartes, Chief Commissioner of Police, and his subordinates were puzzled. They had absolutely no proof whatever to go upon. Nothing came till the third day, when there arrived a letter bearing the Mantua postmark. It was unsigned, undated and unheaded, and written on a long slip torn from the margin of a newspaper. It was simply sealed and addressed and came minus an envelope. As for the letter itself, it was printed by hand in small capitals throughout. It ran thus:

"YOUR EMPEROR IS SAFE AND UNMOLESTED. REST ASSURED THAT THE BODY OF SO BRAVE AND GOOD A MAN IS NOT LIKELY TO RECEIVE ANY INDIGNITY AT OUR HANDS. THE RECOVERY OF THE REMAINS IS A MERE MATTER OF MONEY. ONE HUNDRED THOUSAND GOLD CROWNS IS THE RANSOM DEMANDED, AND NOTHING LESS WILL BE TAKEN. OTHERWISE RUDOLPH CAESAR IS NEVER LIKELY TO REST WITH HIS FATHERS. COMMUNICATIONS IN ANSWER TO THIS WILL ALONE BE ACCEPTED IN THE WAY OF AN ADVERTISEMENT IN THE COLUMNS OF THE ZEITUNG. THEY MUST BE HEADED TO 'CORONET' ONLY."

For a long time did Desartes ponder over this strange letter. If the bona fides of the rascals could be assured, the money would have to be paid, provided always that strategy resulted in failure.

"In any case this letter must be answered," the Count remarked to Wrangel, his next in command. "Let it be announced that we accept the terms, and shall be prepared to pay over the money if we are satisfied that the object we seek will be obtained. See to it at once."

The result of this now brought another letter from the scoundrels. The money difficulty still barred the way. The possession of so large a sum of money in cash was extremely likely to lead to detection. The safeguards proposed by the writer of the letter were stringent. And unless these were complied with, no further communications, could be exchanged.

After a delay of six days, and many fruitless letters, a way out of the difficulty was hit upon. The suggestion was so simple, not to say childish, that Desartes smiled as he perused the ultimatum He might have known that with such men to deal with the simplest and most apparently straightforward plan could really conceal a profundity of cunning and prudence.

To all practical purposes Gryde placed himself unreservedly in Desartes' hands. He assumed that the latter would act honourably towards him: that a secret meeting would take place and the money handed over, when the hiding-place of the late head of the Caesars would be disclosed.

"THE PLACE OF MEETING," Gryde wrote, "WILL BE AN APPARENTLY DESERTED HOUSE IN THE UNTERSTRASSE NO 14. ON FRIDAY NEXT YOUR MESSENGER WILL GET FROM THE BANK IN THE SAME STREET THE NECESSARY MONEY IN GOLD. WE SHALL SEE THAT HE RECEIVES THIS, AND HE WILL PROCEED WITH THE SAME TO NO. 14 IN A CAB. HE WILL KNOCK AT THE DOOR, WHEN A MAN IN LIVERY WILL RECEIVE HIM AND HELP HIM TO CARRY THE GOLD TO A ROOM ON THE GROUND FLOOR. THIS SERVANT WILL BE AN INNOCENT DUPE PROCURED FOR THE OCCASION.

"ALL THIS MUST TAKE PLACE EXACTLY AT FOUR O'CLOCK. IF THE THING IS PROPERLY CARRIED OUT AND NO TREACHERY ATTEMPTED, THE FIVE O'CLOCK POST WILL CONVEY TO COUNT DESARTES THE HIDING-PLACE OF THE DECEASED MONARCH. TO GET AT THE BODY AND RESTORE IT TO ITS PLACE WILL TAKE SOME TIME. ALL THIS TIME THE MESSENGER WITH THE MONEY WILL REMAIN IN NO. 14, BUT AT SEVEN O'CLOCK IN THE EVENING HE WILL BE FREE TO DEPART. IF HE ATTEMPTS TO DO SO BEFORE, HIS HOURS ARE NUMBERED. THIS IS FINAL."

Desartes smiled as he read. He advertised in the Zeitung that all these matters should be carried out faithfully, and up to a certain point he meant all he said.

"We will do it, Wrangel," he said. "The gold shall be procured, and you shall convey the same to No. 14. It shall be the real red gold, and you shall remain there till seven as arranged. Meanwhile a perfect cordon of police shall surround the house, and when the time comes we will take the place and the miscreants as well. This will, of course, be subsequent to the discovery of the Emperor's body. As to the rest I will leave all the arrangements in your very capable hands."

"Your Excellency may be perfectly assured," Wrangel murmured. Whereupon Desartes went tranquilly off to dinner.

It was one o'clock on the eventful Friday, and Gryde was seated in his room awaiting the arrival of Fort. On the table before which he was seated lay a large number of sealed and stamped letters, and a champagne bottle nearly full into which one of those patent screw taps had been inserted. There was a peculiar star on the side of the bottle, suggesting that the same had nearly perished by contact with another hard body, and on the top of the star a spot of wax. But as the champagne exported to Lystria is dipped in wax to the shoulder of the bottle, the fact was not likely to cause attention.

A minute or two later and Fort entered.

"I'm glad you've come," said Gryde.

"All the same, there is nothing further to report. What you have to do is precisely as arranged. You will go to No. 14 at five o'clock precisely and there await the messenger from the bank. Make him open the box and show you the gold, so as to be certain of its being genuine. At a few minutes before seven I will come also—"

"And if the messenger does not arrive?" Fort suggested.

"In that case you will know that treachery is afloat. Therefore you will consult your own safety by staying where you are. Give me the agreed signal from the window and I will put my plan into execution for setting you at liberty. And mind, you are to remain perdu till a quarter to five."

Fort nodded. He was a little puzzled, but at the same time he had a doglike faith in his leader. He would have faced anything for the latter.

"I'll do exactly as you say," he said.

"Good. Now we will have one glass of champagne together, and then I shall turn you out, as I have much to do."

Gryde pressed the lever and a glass of champagne foamed out. As he filled a second glass his forefinger rested on the star on the bottle. The second glass he handed to Fort, and took down the first at one pull.

"Enough for the present," he said. "Now go."

Punctually at four o'clock—exactly an hour before the time arranged for Fort's arrival, strange to say—Wrangel drove up to No. 14 with his burden. As he rang the bell a man replied, and assisted Wrangel to convey his heavy load to a room at the back, then bowed and disappeared.

In the hall Gryde awaited him. None could have recognised him in his disguise.

"You may go now," he said; "my friend has arrived. Here is a gold piece for you."

Scarcely had the door closed behind the dupe when Gryde crept to the room where Wrangel awaited somebody. His back was to Gryde. The latter carried in his hand the weapon somewhat humorously termed a life-preserver. One blow straight and swift under the lobe of the right ear and Wrangel dropped in his tracks like a bullock. In less time than it takes to tell he was gagged and bound and literally rolled into the cellar.

For the next three-quarters of an hour Gryde was busy. He had to transfer the gold to a number of small cases marked "Cycle Bearings" and consigned to a certain house in the neighbourhood of Fenchurch Street, London. The back of the house opened upon a narrow, dingy lane faced by a blank wall of a factory. As Gryde got the last of his cases into the lane a waggon lumbered along.

"Here," Gryde cried, "you're late, you know. Get these boxes aboard. As I'm going the same way I'll ride with you to the station."

The driver made no objection to a fellow working man accompanying him. And thus it came about that Gryde personally superintended the dispatch of his treasure per passenger train, and a few minutes after Fort's arrival at No. 14 was on his way to the frontier in the same train as the precious metal. A workman lounged in the corner of a third-class carriage. Who would have identified him as being the author of the most sensational crime known in modern Europe?

Meanwhile Fort waited and waited doggedly. A clock somewhere struck seven. At the same moment the front door opened and heavy feet tramped in. Fort was on the alert in an instant. That he had been betrayed never occurred to the brave ruffian for a moment.

He knew that he would have to fight for his life. He set his teeth hard and faced the ring of police who had sprung upon him. He had no weapon. He sprang forward with the courage and force of despair. An instant later he was struggling and fighting with the strength of a tiger.

Then his strength seemed suddenly to relax, he fell back helplessly into the arms of one of his captors. A blue tinge came over his face; the side of his mouth drew up in a horribly grotesque manner. A shudder and shiver, and Fort had escaped. He was dead.

Almost before the police could realise what had happened, Desartes came, hurrying in. His air was elated. His eyes sparkled with triumph.

"The rascals told the truth," he exclaimed. "The Emperor has been found concealed in a stone coffin in the vaults below the cathedral. We had a long search for the body. The miscreants removed it by the way of the grating behind the bier. You have the man, and you have recovered the money as well."

One of the police explained the new feature of the drama. A search was made, but no gold could be found, nothing but Wrangel in the cellar groaning pitifully and anathematising what had happened. But gold there was none, and to this day the hiding-place of the same is wrapped in mystery. That they had obtained possession of the leading villain in the cast, Desartes never doubted. And he had escaped them.

And in the fulness of time Gryde read the "solution" of the mystery comfortably in London. He had his money, he had come out of the danger unscathed. He had coolly and in cold blood betrayed his colleague to save himself, for the champagne had been poisoned to make assurance doubly sure.

"And how ridiculously easy it was after all," the master scoundrel muttered as he flung his paper aside. "What a success, too, were those gelatine bombs, exploded by the force of their fall. Neat and not destructive. Police! I could rob the Bank of England itself, and trace the crime to Scotland Yard. Maybe I will some day, before I settle down to growing orchids and courting the gods of the bourgeoisie."

AT WINDSOR

CHAPTER I

The Mahrajah of Curriebad was for the present located in Jermyn Street. On the following day he was commanded to Windsor for the regulation dinner; in the meantime he had practically chartered the hotel.

Morals the Mahrajah possessed none—they would have been perfectly superfluous in any case—but money he had in plenty. For this reason the India Office people were fond of him.

At the present moment they were desirous of getting something out of their distinguished visitor: more territory, more men, an extra sack of diamonds; and the Windsor interview was expected to clinch the business. Meantime the dusky potentate winked the other eye. He fully appreciated the meaning of the phrase. He had a private music-hall of his own at Curriebad.

Incidentally it may be mentioned that a more consummate rascal than Nana Rau never drew the breath of life through shifty lips. Of his early career people knew but little. They noted that he spoke excellent English, and that his knowledge of the Stud-Book was not of a perfunctory character.

Nana Rau had just dined alone. As he lighted his second cigarette a servant entered with the announcement that a visitor waited below. With rare graciousness the Prince ordered the gentleman to be conveyed into his presence.

He came, he bowed, he closed the door behind him.

"My name is Wilfred Vaughan, your Highness," he said.

The potentate nodded. The stranger prepossessed him, he was so exquisitely dressed.

"Sit down, Mr. Vaughan," he said, "and take a cigarette. Then, if you please, you can proceed to unfold your business."

"I am obliged to you. Ah, what it is to be an Eastern Potentate! Now, it would be impossible for me to get cigarettes like these. My good friend, it is possible that you have forgotten the old Oxford days?"

"That is a long time ago—twenty years," Nana Rau replied, uneasily.

He felt uneasy, too. The India Office would have been surprised to hear that Nana Rau had ever been at Oxford. But then he was not Nana Rau at all, and four good lives stood between him and the sacks of Curriebad diamonds. Also incidents had happened at Oxford which it was expedient should remain buried in the silent tomb with the flowers blooming atop, and no white stone to mark their memory. Even now, were those stories told, Nana Rau knew that his connection with the throne of Curriebad would come to an abrupt conclusion.

"Twenty years are nothing," Vaughan said sententiously, "and my memory is good."

"You are Vaughan of 'The House,' of course. What can you remember?"

"Well, for instance," Vaughan smiled, "there was a pretty tobacconist's assistant: she was found dead under very suspicious circumstances. About the same time an Indian student at Christ Church disappeared. The police were anxious to find him—very anxious. Strange to say he was never heard of again; and, until to-day, I haven't seen him since."

Nana Rau recovered his equanimity. His thin lips ceased to twitch. He felt that this was a mere matter of money.

"Old chap," he said quite cordially, "what's the figure?"

"You always were a sensible man," Vaughan replied. "Never any dashed Oriental poetry about you. All the same, there is no figure—in money signs, that is."

"Then what the deuce do you want?"

"That I can hardly go into in detail. Let us speak plainly. I've got the whip hand of you: a few words from me and your interest in the sovereign lord and ruler business stops. You recognise that, of course. That I require something is obvious. I want you to stay away from Windsor to-morrow."

Nana Rau smiled at the suggestion.

"Absurd," he said; "you know I dare not do so."

"Under ordinary circumstances, no. But these are not ordinary circumstances. You are merely going semi-officially. There will be no State fuss; you will dine at the Castle, and return here next morning. What is intended to take place yonder you know as well as I do."

"I don't want to go. It's certain to be deuced slow. And if you can only show me some way out of the difficulty without compromising myself—"

"Of course I have my plans prepared," Vaughan interrupted.

"You don't leave Paddington till a train somewhere about six. Here is my card with my address. My place is out at Epsom. Come out there and lunch with me to-morrow, and bring your suite with you, baggage and all, and if we can't come to terms, my carriage shall take you to Paddington."

"I have only two chaps with me besides my cook," said the Prince.

"Good. So much the better. Then you will come?"

"Well, there is no harm in that," said Nana Rau. "I will."

A few minutes later Wilfred Vaughan, alias Felix Gryde, was placidly walking along Piccadilly. He turned into the Café Soyer, where the other parties to the conspiracy were awaiting him and dinner. They were the tools to be used and to be discarded when the curtain fell.

"It's all right," Gryde proceeded to explain over the bisque. "I told you Nana Rau was the same man I used to be at Oxford with twenty years ago. I spotted him at Ascot, and I never forget a face. Nana was terribly frightened, and, indeed, it was no idle boast that I could bring about his ruin."

"Will he come?" asked tht second conspirator.

"And will the original plan stand?" asked the third.

"Exactly as arranged. You will look after all the details, as I shall be very busy till luncheon time to-morrow. You will see that the cold luncheon is properly laid out by the local caterer, and pay for it. Then the keys must be packed up so as to be posted to the landlord's agent directly we leave the house. Let the carriage be ordered for 3.30 prompt, and pay the liveryman for that also. Let it be understood that we have just taken the house for six months furnished— which is, indeed, the fact—and go to a registry office to inquire about servants. Order a dozen, and say the housekeeper will call to interview them on a certain day. Each of us, till the time for changing comes, retains his present disguise."

As a "make-up" artist Gryde had no equal. Several society acquaintances there passed him without a s:gn of recognition.

"That's all very well," suggested one of the lieutenants; "but suppose any of the Castle people happen to have seen Nana Rau?"

"Which they haven't done," said Gryde. "I have made the most minute inquiries on this head. Besides, one Eastern Potentate is as like another as two peas when he is in his full war paint. It's any money nobody yonder speaks the language, and if they do I shall make it my pleasure to stick to English. As you have both presumably been in England before, you can do the same. You have carefully studied the plans of the apartments I gave to you?"

The others protested that they had.

"Very good," Gryde concluded; "in that case there is no more to be said. We ought to find enough within easy reach yonder to reward us for all our trouble. And the servants of the sovereign shall assist us in getting it away. I hope you won't find it altogether too slow."

Gryde settled the score and they rose to depart. In the street they separated, and each took a different way. Then they went to bed early and virtuously as befit men who have before them matters of importance on the morrow. On the whole they slept better than Nana Rau, Mahrajah of Curriebad.

CHAPTER II

It was with considerable misgivings that Nana Rau drove with two dusky assistants down to Epsom the following morning.

With him was all his baggage, a formidable-looking amount for a night out; but then the dazzling splendour of Eastern attire cannot be measured by Western sartorial restrictions. These big trunks contained the full war paint which Nana Rau and suite intended to don after luncheon, and ere proceeding to Windsor.

One thing Nana Rau was fully resolved upon. Nothing should induce him to play into "Vaughan's" hands unless the latter could provide him with a proper way out of the difficulty. It was only natural that the Prince should desire to protect himself, and nothing short of being able to show that he was the innocent victim of a vile conspiracy would satisfy him.

The Indians reached Vaughan's hospitable mansion at length and were met at the door by that individual himself.

"I am afraid I shall have to request you to dispense with a deal of ceremony," he said. "The fact is, this place has been let furnished for about a year, and my late tenants only turned out of it last week, and thus we are terribly short of servants. These footmen don't seem able to do anything without a lot of women to help them."

Vaughan, or Gryde rather, rang the bell violently, and presently a pair of men-servants appeared breathlessly. They were a fine-looking pair of men, and their livery left nothing to be desired. The astute reader will have little difficulty in guessing who these footmen were.

"Whatever have you fellows been doing?" Gryde demanded.

"Please, sir," replied one, in the purest of Cockney accents, "it's all along of the new cook, which she's drunk—"

Gryde waved these details aside.

"I desire to know nothing of these matters," he replied. "Take the Prince up to the room prepared for him, and these gentlemen also, and see that they have everything they require. Luncheon is prepared, I suppose?"

"Luncheon is waiting in the dining-room now, sir."

A little later and Nana Rau, together with his host and attendants, sat down to one of the most perfect luncheons it is possible to imagine. The Prince was a bit of an epicure in his way, and as the meal proceeded he softened. The choice champagne rendered him indifferent to the calls of Windsor. And really, it seemed quite bad taste to stand in the light of so enlightened a bon vivant as Vaughan.

Absolutely nothing had been left undone. The luncheon was a work of art, the wines were cameos in their way, and the waiting of the two confederates left nothing to be desired. In the poetic language of the modern Babylon, Nana Rau was an accomplished "tiddler"; in the old days he would have been a three-bottle man, and to leave such a feast of alcohol for a mere Court function partook almost of the nature of a crime.

"Then why leave it?" Gryde asked, when the attendants had withdrawn and he and the Prince were alone. "Stay and make an evening of it."

"What's the good of talking that dashed nonsense?" said Nana Rau thickly. "You know as well as possible that I must go."

"But it was arranged that I was to take your place."

"O! I know that's your game. I suppose you've got some diplomatic swindle on. Only show me a clear way out—a way which will absolutely absolve me from all blame—and you shall take my place with pleasure."

"I am about to do so," said Gryde.

"I think I shall be able to satisfy even your scruples if you will permit me to leave you for a minute."

Nana Rau waved his hand majestically. He wanted no other company beyond that superb champagne. He closed his eyes with the ecstasy of it He opened them again with a start five minutes later. Then, with a beatific smile upon his face, he slipped from his chair on to the floor and slept.

Let no slur rest upon the fair fame of Nana Rau. For instance, he was a great deal more sober than Mr. Pickwick when discovered in the village pound. But even the strongest of heads cannot rise superior to a bottle or so of '74 champagne plus a narcotic of potent properties.

A minute or two later Gryde entered the room, followed by his two "footmen."

"You fellows did your part uncommonly well," Gryde said. "The Christy minstrel on the floor is firm enough, and so are the others. They are perfectly safe here until this time to-morrow. Now then, boys— no time to be lost. Let us go upstairs at once and get the Eastern robes on. Very nice to think that we should be actually provided with our disguises."

The work was by no means easy, though Gryde was an artist so far as this branch of his profession was concerned. But patience and skill overcomes all things, and at length the task was accomplished. It would indeed have puzzled an Englishman to have told the counterfeit from the originals.

"This thing will make a bit of a stir," said Gryde.

"Egad, you are right there," said one of the others, grimly. "Look here, Mr. Vaughan, I'm not very particular, but I have jibbed a bit over this job. Any ordinary woman in England, but when it comes to—"

"You seem to regard me as somewhat simple," Gryde interrupted. "Do you suppose I should be guilty of anything in such fearful taste?"

"But I was under the impression that we were going down on purpose to—"

"So we are. But my words will come true all the same. At six o'clock this evening important information, bearing upon the face of it every evidence of truth, will reach the India Office. A certain great lady will be informed of the same without delay. And Nana Rau will not kiss the hand of her to whom he owes fealty."

The scrupulous one said no more, being quite satisfied with this explanation.

A little later a resplendent carriage drove up to the house, and the three Indians gravely emerged. Two of them stood aside and bowed low as Gryde passed, and then, when the two huge trunks were hoisted on the carriage, they entered.

The journey to Paddington was made without incident. Gryde had laid his plans so carefully, he had made so many inquiries beforehand, that he has nothing to fear from any display of ignorance on his part.

Everything went well, the retained carriage was entered at length, and the train started.

"Nothing wanting," said Gryde, with an air of satisfaction; "not a single hitch—and, really, this is a most critical part of the performance. They might have laid a strip of crimson carpet across the platform, but at times like these one is not disposed to be hypercritical. Windsor will be the next trouble."

But Windsor proved no bother at all. The red liveried servants were allowed to take everything in their own hands, and ere long the adventurers found themselves bowling along the wide avenues up to the Castle.

"How do you feel?" asked Gryde.

"Uncommonly nervous," said the others in chorus.

Gryde smiled. He did not appear to be suffering from the same malady. On the contrary, he was perfectly at his ease.

"The great charm of this mode of life," he muttered," lies in the fact that it never lacks variety."

CHAPTER III

As far astheir reception was concerned, even the sensitive mind of an Indian could find nothing at which to take offence. It was, of course, with profound regret that the pseudo Nana Rau heard that no visitors could be expected at the royal table the same evening in consequence of a slight indisposition on the part of a certain great ruler. Nor was it suggested by the gorgeous official who conducted the interview that the visit of the Prince should be prolonged in consequence.

"It is greatly to be regretted," Nana murmured.

"I can assure you that the regret is mutual," was the reply. "If the Prince will honour us by dining with the Household, together with his suite"

"I shall be delighted," the Prince interpolated. "As to my suite, they had better dine in the apartment apportioned to their use. Afterwards you will greatly oblige me by letting an attendant conduct them over the state rooms, and show them some of the treasures of this wonderful place. It is a pleasure that my faithful followers have looked forward to for a long time."

"Everything shall be done to make them comfortable," the big official replied. "May I remind the Prince that we dine at eight."

Nana Rau nodded carelessly and intimated his desire to be alone with his men. The request was immediately granted. For a little time the three conspirators stood as far from the door as possible talking in whispers.

"You see how beautifully things are falling out," said Gryde. "We are here without any suspicion being aroused. There is no chance of public sentiment being awakened by a flagrant insult to the sovereign. All we have to do is to fill these big trunks in the still watches of the night, and get these good people to convey them to the station for us in the morning. By way of spotting all the things worth having, an attendant will take you round presently and point out the plums to you. But I need not waste my time on advice; you are both capital judges of articles of value."

"And as to you?"

"As to me, I dine with the Household. Of course, you both occupy my dressing-room. We leave by a train about seven, as I have an engagement in Manchester to fill to-morrow night, or, at least, the real Nana has, so we shall be away before anything is missing."

"And if things are missed just after we start?"

"What matter? We should be the last to be suspected. And you may be certain the common or garden police would never be consulted in a matter like this. Absolutely nothing in the way of a public scandal would be permitted. And say they looked like bringing it home to us. Would they care to stop us, and cart us off to a police-station? Not a bit of it. Am I not a man of power in our country? A trustworthy courtier would come to us with every expression of regret to call for the few trifles that were by mistake taken away with our luggage. But as we are not going to Jermyn Street, and as we shall emerge on Paddington platform clothed and in our right minds, they have little chance of seeing those treasures again."

There was sound logic in every word that Gryde uttered. Unless by any chance, and that was indeed a remote one, the real Indian was discovered, they were absolutely safe. But, even if by some strange fortune the Simon Pure was unearthed, the powerful drug would seal his lips for some hours yet.

It was, therefore, with an easy conscience and a mind at rest that Nana Rau went down to dine with the Household. He would have felt a little more comfortable, perhaps, in ordinary evening dress, but nobody seemed to notice this. At the same time he had the satisfaction of knowing that there was positively no flaw in his attire, and all the more so because at least two generals who knew India well were present.

Gryde said very little, and that little awkwardly. His cue was to do the shy and slightly suspicious guest, which part he acted to perfection.

A little before eleven he deemed it prudent to retire. In that exalted of all exalted spheres they are not particularly late, and by twelve o'clock sleep brooded over the Castle.

But not in the two rooms devoted to the Indian guests. They sat waiting and talking there for the critical moment to arrive, which hour had been fixed by Gryde for two. Meantime they had to wait.

"You have seen everything?" Gryde murmured.

"Well, not everything," was the reply; "but enough, and more than enough. We can take away thousands of pounds' worth of stuff without quitting this floor."

"So much the better," Gryde replied with a smile. "Never run any unnecessary risks. Not that it would matter very much if one of you were taken." The time crept slowly on, and at length the hour came. Gryde jumped to his feet. He was alert and eager enough now. There was no need for lights, as all the passages gleamed. What they had to fear were the watchmen. But there were three of them.

"Now follow me," Gryde whispered. There was no time for hesitation. The corridors appeared to be silent and deserted, but at any time a watchman might come along. But nothing happened to disturb the work of the adventurers. Tapestry hangings and Cordova leather here and there not only looked patrician and valuable, but they formed capital cover for a laden thief whose modesty is in proportion to the value of his burden.

At the end of an hour Gryde's bedroom presented an appearance of dazzling splendour. Most of the treasures collected were not only historic but of immense intrinsic value. On the whole, the haul was perhaps a better one than the theft of the regal corpse.

Even Gryde was satisfied at length.

"No more," he said. "Now remove those bars of lead from the baggage and hide them behind the curtains. Pack the stuff away quietly and then get to bed. We shall have to be up a little after six, remember."

Shortly after seven the next morning three shivering Orientals were sped away from the Castle by a big official, who strove politely to hide his yawns. When the station was reached and the Orientals were alone they developed new vigour. One of them even went so far as to see the baggage safely in the van. Perhaps he mistrusted the absent guard, for he followed it in, the others standing by th« door.

His movements were peculiar and rapid. He touched a spring on each box and the basket frames fell all to pieces. These were immediately hidden under mail bags. Three huge portmanteaux of different colour were revealed. To each of these a label bearing a different name was attached; the baggage was quite transformed.

Then the shivering Orientals went on their way to the carriage reserved for them. Directly they were inside the blinds were pulled down. The loose Eastern robes were discarded, and beneath them were disclosed three typical English garbs—a parson's, a country squire's, and that of a man about town. With the free use of the lavatory and a make-up box produced by Gryde, he and the other artists were utterly changed by the time Slough was reached. Just before then a big bundle was carefully dropped out of the window. The train pulled up at Slough. Gryde opened the window opposite the platform.

"Now," he whispered, "you've all got your tickets?"

Confederates One and Two nodded curtly. An instant later the door was closed again with the curtains still down, and the trio had reached the further platform without attracting the slightest attention. When they strolled back again by the proper way to the train they appeared to be strangers to each other, for each entered a different carriage, not, needless to remark, the one with the drawn blinds. Then the train sped on towards Paddington.

Once arrived there, Gryde was out of the carriage before the train had fairly stopped. In this move the other actors were not far behind him. The great object now was to secure the baggage and get it out of the station without delay. Out came the stuff tumbling on the platform, and a moment later the three precious portmanteaux were hoisted upon three cabs and all driven away at once to separate destinations. The coup had been accomplished!

But not with much to spare. As Gryde looked with lamb-like gaze over the tops of his glasses, a parson to the life, he saw coming down the slope into the station two quiet men, who appeared to see nothing. Gryde smiled.

"They've found it out and telegraphed," he chuckled, "or else two shining lights like Marsh and Elliott would not have been put on the job. If they have found Nana Rau, why we have no time to lose. If not, why so much the better."

It was about nine o'clock the same evening, and the three conspirators, absolutely without disguise, and qua Gryde and Co., were seated over dinner in the former's rooms. They had the air of men who had done well and virtuously

"You managed to get rid of your lot?" Gryde asked.

"Yes," the first man responded. "All beyond recognition by this time. You'll see to the disposal?"

"I suppose you are all right?" Gryde said to the other.

"I am also satisfied," said he. "We both deposited the plunder as you directed. Most of my stuff was jewelled, and you can't recognise jewels. We are as safe as houses. For my part I should like to have a bit of a rest, considering that I haven't seen my own natural face for a fortnight. When I look at myself in the glass I feel quite startled."

"Let's go round to a restaurant," suggested Gryde, " and see if anything's come out."

The proposal found favour in the eyes of the others. In the St. Giles's one or two men were languidly discussing something in connection with Windsor Castle and incidentally Indian princes.

"What's that?" Gryde demanded.

"All in the Globe," said an exhausted voice. "Rum case, by Jove!"

Gryde took up the special Globe and turned it over languidly. He had hardly' expected to find the case public. But all the same it was, and nothing had been lost in the display of the juicy item:

BURGLARY AT WINDSOR CASTLE
INGENIOUS AND SUCCESSFUL FRAUD
AN INDIAN PRINCE IS DRUGGED AND IMPERSONATED BY THIEVES

From information just received it is evident that last night a clever and successful attempt at burglary was carried out at Windsor Castle.

It appears that H.R.H. the Mahrajah of Curriebad was summoned to Windsor for some purpose of State, and this seems to have been known to the miscreants. The Prince was lured away to Epsom by an individual claiming to be an old friend of his, the pretext being an invitation to luncheon. There he and his attendants were drugged and locked in a deserted house whilst the pseudo Indians repaired to Windsor.

What happened there we are not in a position to say, but early this morning the Prince and his attendants escaped from their prison-house, and lost no time in laying the case before the proper authorities. The police are extremely reticent upon the point, but we have the best authority for saying that during the night the daring thieves carried away from Windsor articles to the value of thousands of pounds. How they managed to get clear away is a mystery, for though the sham Indians were seen to enter their reserved carriage at Windsor, it is certain they did not detrain en route. Up to the present nothing has been heard or seen of them.

At the last moment we are informed that a large bundle of Oriental robes have been picked up on the line near Slough. How they got there must for the present remain a mere matter for conjecture.

Gryde smiled as he laid the paper aside.

"Looks to me like a hoax," he said,

"Depend upon it, our friend the Mahrajah got screwed and imagined the whole thing. Burglary at Windsor Castle! The whole thing is too absurd."

With which Gryde went off to play pool, at which game, as usual, he proved singularly successful. But he declined to stay late.

"No," he said; "I was up nearly all night. Some other time, perhaps. But you chaps may depend upon it those 'Indians' will never be caught. See you fellows in a day or two. I'm going out of town to-morrow for a time."

But Gryde's tools never saw him again. They had pooled their plunder, and Gryde was to dispose of it. Yet days and weeks went by, and like the raven,

"Still is sitting, never flitting,"

they tarried for the master who came not.

"Some day," growled No. 1, "we shall meet Vaughan again; then let him look to himself. I should know him anywhere."

Vain boast, fond delusion. Tools it was necessary for Gryde to have, but as to using them and making familiar as Gryde with them—never! A myth was "Vaughan," and as a myth he is likely to remain.

THE SILVERPOOL CUP

CHAPTER I

Sackville Mayne was still sober, although it was nearly two. The marble clock in the Mornington Arms Hotel recorded the hour and the phenomenon. Years of vinous environment has not yet robbed Mayne of the manorial air, although the necessary acres for the part were gone long ago.

Neither had Mayne quite lost the art of dining. He had done ample justice to the dinner presented by his peripatetic host the Duke de Cavour. The wines left nothing to be desired.

"I am charmed," said the Duke in quite passable English, "charmed to have met you again. Our last foregathering in Naples was many years ago."

For Mayne's part he had forgotten the incident entirely. The Duke's memory was evidently more trustworthy than his own. All Mayne knew was that he had been in Naples at the time his noble host had mentioned. The latter, an elderly buck with small eyes and a ludicrous pointed moustache, nodded over his glass.

"Those were pleasant days," he said, "twenty years ago! Dear me! And yet when I saw you in the billiard room last night I recognised you instantly. And what horses you used to drive in those days!"

Mayne smiled. The Duke had touched him on a tender spot. As the fond mother clings to the reprobate son who spells the family ruin, so did Mayne still love the equine flesh which had been his destruction.

"I've come down in the world," he said. "Egad, how I manage to live upon my paltry little place is a mystery even to myself. But I still continue to have a bit of blood about me. It isn't every man who can boast of having bred and run two Derby winners."

"The old Godolphin blood, I presume?" suggested the Duke.

Mayne nodded. There was a bond of union between himself and his host. All he knew about the latter he had gleaned that day from the Almanach de Gotha. The exclusive volume in question recorded the fact that de Cavour was an enthusiast where racing was concerned. In a hazy kind of way, he wondered what so great a man was doing in Mornington.

"You race still?" the Duke asked.

"Oh no, I can't afford it. I only wish I could. I've got a colt entered for the Royal Clarendon Stakes at Oldmarket— run-off next week, you know—but I shall have to forfeit. Bar Sinister can beat any horse in the race bar the favourite—ay, and even beat Rialto too, if wound up."

"Come, my friend, you are not so poor as all that."

Mayne smiled into his glass. Good wine develops the philosophical side of a man's nature. It also taps the well-springs of confidence.

"Indeed I am," he said; "and yet with a little capital, I think I could see my way clear. I would sell my soul for £1,000."

"Men are prepared to take big risks for sums like that."

"I know it. I am prepared to undertake anything short of manslaughter."

The Duke paused in the manipulation of a cigarette in his slim fingers. For an elderly, gouty gentleman with a suggestion of apoplexy in the region of the carotid, he had remarkably clean sinewy hands.

"I can show you how to make £1,000 with no risk at all," he said quietly. "All you have to do is to take the money and hold your tongue."

"How pleasant! And the conditions?"

"Nothing more than the loan of your colt Bar Sinister. You will permit me to find the money for the stakes, and the horse will be sent up to-morrow to a stable I shall mention, and in due course he will win the Royal Clarendon."

"Without a month's preparation the thing is impossible."

The Duke smiled. There was a strange light in his beady eyes.

"There is many a slip, of course," he responded. "Anyway, it matters very little whether Bar Sinister wins or not. That is a mere detail in my scheme. The question is, can I have the horse if I deposit the money?"

"Now you ask the question, of course you may."

"Good. Mind, this is a profound secret. The horse is to be sent to Oldmarket to Gunter's stables to run in your name. Whether Bar Sinister wins or not matters very little. The favourite is firmly established at even money, so if I were you I should not back the colt."

Mayne nodded carelessly. It was not for him to suggest that some rascality was afloat. He had known in his time racing dukes with no more inherent morality than dustmen. "It's all the same to me," he said, "as long as I get the money. By the way, on the day following the Clarendon, the cup is run for at Silverpool. Haven't you got something starting there?"

"A horse of my own breeding," the Duke responded. "Confetti. No chance, I fear. The odds are forty to one against. Only a few personal friends know I am in England, or perhaps the odds would be a little less. You will see to this matter at once."

Mayne gave the desired assurance. Then the Duke proceeded to take from his pocket notes to the value of one thousand pounds.

"I am going to Oldmarket in the morning," he explained, "but not as the Duke de Cavour. I have my reasons for being known as Mr. Smith. If you desire to communicate with me please do so in that name per Gunter. Again let me urge upon you the advantage of silence in this matter."

A little while later and Mayne was driving his weedy bay towards his place which lay just outside Mornington. Meanwhile, the Duke de Cavour alias Smith had retired to his private sitting-room. Once there he lighted a cigarette and locked the door. With a quasi-magical sweep of his hand, he removed wig and moustache, and stood confessed for the time being in the legitimate form of Felix Gryde.

"Now let me see how I stand," he muttered, throwing himself into a chair. "I am the Duke de Cavour. In my disguise, made up from personal inspection of the distinguished individual in question, I could defy the noble mother of de Cavour to tell the difference between us. For the present the genuine article is under private restraint in Genoa. That is a fact of which the world knows nothing. To make matters still more safe, there is no need for me to appear personally, except at the finish to draw the money from the turf commissioners; and nobody will know that the horse running as Confetti in the Silverpool Cup is anything but de Cavour's colt. One way and another I ought to make £100,000 out of this business; and I deserve it, for the scheme has occupied all my care and attention for a whole year."

So saying Gryde rose and proceeded to unlock a dispatch box, and took from thence two large photographs. They were both likenesses of horses and appeared to be taken from the same plate. Gryde regarded them long and earnestly.

"A wonderful resemblance." he said, "the same age to a month, the same marks, the same everything. It's the Godolphin blood in both, I expect. Upon my word, I don't know which is Mayne's Bar Sinister, and which is the favourite for the Grand Clarendon, Sir George Julyan's Rialto. I wonder what Mayne would say if he knew I had been hanging about here for six weeks to get that photograph. And what a coup this is going to be!"

CHAPTER II

Oldmarket, as everybody knows, is the headquarters of the racing world. There are many training establishments there, from the palatial concern with its hundreds of hands down to the tiny quarters from whence from time to time a "dark horse" emerges, and some Tom Jones springs into sudden prominence, and thenceforth is respectfully spoken of by equine scribes as Mr. Thomas Jones.

Such an establishment was Gunter's, which boasted a tumble-down house, and a row of ill-found stables tenanted for the most part by platers. Gunter and two lads found themselves quite equal to the task set before them.

Gunter was a typical specimen of his class, sharp, dapper, and cunning, and good enough for anything outside the pale of the law. On the night following the little dinner at Mornington, Gunter sat in his shabby parlour, a rank cigar in his mouth—a tumbler of gin and water before him.

On the other side of the table was a foxy-looking man, dressed like a stud groom, and whom Gunter addressed with grudging civility as Mr. Smith. We have seen him before under the guise of the Duke de Cavour.

"I suppose it is all right?" asked the latter.

"Oh, it's all right up to now" Gunter replied dubiously. "Bar Sinister came in the dusk clothed up to the eyes, and I stored him into a loose box at once. I took care that the lads didn't see too much."

"You've got them out of the way, of course?"

"Yes, they won't be back till morning. Your part of the business satisfactory?"

"Perfectly. Don't you be afraid over me. Within a fortnight's time you will have your pockets full of money, and I shall be back on my way to Australia again the richer for the coup. You see I don't show up at all—merely a horse of mine goes from this stable to run for the Silverpool Cup. The Duke de Cavour is not known in English sporting circles, and nobody takes an interest in him. It's quite safe, because there really is such a man, and at present he is under restraint—don't you hear? It doesn't matter what name I take in my betting against Rialto for the Grand Clarendon on Friday so long as I have satisfied my commissioner of my bona fides. I have employed a different commissioner to put my money on Confetti for the Silverpool."

"And if they find out that your Confetti is really—"

"How can they? Confetti has never appeared in public yet. Still, the likeness between the two horses is so wonderful that I am not particularly uneasy. Now you have a good look at the colt? You know Rialto, of course?"

"What do you think? Do I know my own mother?"

"Very good. Then come to the stables and let us see that everything is quite in order."

Gunter followed with a lantern. In one of the stalls stood a handsome dark chestnut clothed to the eyes, the clothes, strange to say, marked in blue with the monogram "G.J."—nothing less, in fact, than Sir George Julyan's copyright The set had been stolen from the owner of the favourite for the Grand Clarendon for a purpose which will be disclosed in due course.

The chestnut was stripped, and for some time Smith and Gunter stood contemplating him from all points of view.

"It is a wonderful likeness to Rialto," Gunter exclaimed. "If you'd searched the world you would not have found a better match."

"It has taken me nearly a year to do it," Smith replied.

"Well, you look like getting your money back, sir. If I could only see the next two hours safely over, why—"

"Leave that to me," responded the other sternly. "Everything is ready. You have managed to get a key to fit the back entrance to Lorrimer's stable?"

Gunter nodded. Lorrimer's was a big establishment close at hand where Sir George Julyan's horses were trained, and where Rialto, the favourite for the Grand Clarendon, lay at the present moment.

Then Smith addressed his colleague long and earnestly. The latter followed every word carefully. When the hour of midnight struck the lights were put out and the stable door gently opened. It was pitch dark then, but it made no difference to Gunter. He could have found his way for a radius of a mile blindfold. The turf was thick and yielding underfoot, so that the adventurers made no noise. They were not alone, for Gunter was leading Bar Sinister by the bridle. Silently they made their way across the heath to a spot where a clump of trees were faintly outlined. These were not far from Lorrimer's stables. The journey was made without a single soul being encountered.

The critical moment had arrived—Smith, or to call him by his proper name, Felix Gryde, peered into the darkness. Not more than a hundred yards away from him he could make out Lorrimer's stables.

Gunter fairly shivered with excitement. Rogue and big as he was, this was the first scheme in which had entered the element of personal danger.

"Now you stay here perfectly still till you hear me whistle," Gryde said sternly; "and when I do so, bring the horse forward. Don't show up yourself, the idea being to lead these people to believe that Rialto has found his way out of the stable."

Gunter muttered something, and Gryde disappeared. He came at length to the buildings and proceeded to skirt round them till the far side was reached. Here he stopped and listened intently. Not a sound was to be heard from the semi-detached building where the favourite for the Royal Clarendon was quartered. Then Gryde stepped into the outer box, opening the door by means of a key. There was plenty of straw littering the floor, which Gryde proceeded to moisten with the aid of a jar of paraffin with which he had armed himself for the purpose.

All remained perfectly still. No sound came from the room over the box where the favourite lay beyond a tough snore. The head lad in charge of Rialto had evidently dropped into a sound slumber.

"I hope he won't sleep too long," Gryde chuckled.

The next proceeding was to advance into the box devoted to the pampered quadruped. To fix blinkers over the animal's eyes was a sufficiently delicate job, but it was at length accomplished.

Then the far stable door was just opened. A match was laid to the saturated straw and a brilliant tongue of flame shot up. In less time than it takes to tell the whole place was roaring and crackling.

Two minutes were allowed to lapse and then Gryde crept into the open. He commenced to hammer on the walls and to yell "Fire" at the top of his voice.

From an uneasy dream the head lad was aroused. Scared and frightened he stumbled down the ladder and bolted out for his life. Before the occupants of the other boxes were aroused, Gryde had passed into the stable again. There was still room for a clear passage for the horse. It was just touch and go, but Gryde coaxed the frightened animal out and led it away into the darkness. An instant later and a shrill whistle rang out on the air.

By this time quite a small mob of helpers had arrived.

Buckets were procured, and amongst much noise and clatter the fire was extinguished. But what had become of the horse? No sooner had this question commenced to pass from lip than a pair of ears sharper than the rest discerned the sound of hoofs.

"Here's the tit," yelled a voice from the darkness, "standin' here like a lamb. Blest if I ever see such a knowing creature."

The head lad gave a sigh of relief.

"Thank goodness!" he muttered. "Here, Joe, go and turn those colts out of the far box yonder and get Rialto in at once."

Apparently the horse was none the worse for his adventure. He appeared to be unhurt down to the last row of braid upon his blanket. That anything was wrong, that the affair was anything but an accident, nobody dreamed.

Meanwhile Gryde with his prize had slipped away to an appointed spot, where he waited patiently till everything had passed off quietly. At the end of an hour Gunter approached with the greatest caution.

"Ah, I see you've got him," he whispered.

"Of course I have. How did you get on?"

"Splendidly," Gunter replied. "They never saw me at all, and they took Bar Sinister for their own Rialto as naturally as possible; and I'll lay a wager that not one of them will ever know the difference. In all the years I've been in this line, I never saw such a likeness."

"You are right there," said Gryde.

"But hadn't we better get Rialto back to our own stable without further delay?"

A little later, and Rialto stood in the place where Bar Sinister recently was. The two men watched him with admiration.

"The finest colt in England and the best three-year-old to-day," Gryde exclaimed. "But he isn't going to be Rialto or Bar Sinister any longer. Your lads haven't seen him stripped, you say, so they haven't a notion what he is like. Now then, you boast that you can 'fake' a horse better than any man in England. Let us see you get rid of those white stockings and star, in fact turn the finely trained Rialto into the half wound Confetti—the Confetti who is to land me such a coup over the Silverpool Cup."

Gunter chuckled hoarsely.

"Don't you worry," he said. "Confetti won't gain a friend when he's pulled out for the preliminary canter on Monday, and he'll win in a canter. Go and smoke a cigar in my room and leave me for a couple of hours. When you come back, I shall be able to astonish you."

All the same it was nearly daylight when Gunter summoned Gryde to see the result of his handiwork. He held up the lantern with artistic pride.

"There," he laughed hoarsely, "what do you think of that?"

Gryde expressed his satisfaction, as well he might. Gone were the white stockings and the star, gone was the sleek and glossy coat. The difference in the appearance of the colt was wonderful. He was transformed into another animal.

"Looks ragged and half trained," Gunter chuckled. "Suggests speed, but a little thick, perhaps. They'll open their eyes a bit up yonder when he spreadeagles his field for the Silverpool. He's simply chucked in at the weight."

An extremely fashionable crowd had assembled at Oldmarket the following afternoon to witness the race for the Grand Clarendon. Royalty was present, and the stands were packed with fair women and brave men. Amongst the latter, perfectly at home and yet apart from the rest, was a neatly attired individual, who, had he been asked his name, would have answered to that of Smith. He lolled over the railings in front of the enclosure, a cigarette in his well-gloved fingers. Any sportsman of note would have passed his get-up approvingly, and yet there was nothing about the man to attract attention—he seemed to fit quite naturally into the picture.

Probably the least excited spectator present when the horses were weighed out for the Grand Clarendon was this Smith, otherwise Gryde. Close behind him were a lot of superb sporting dandies, conspicuous amongst them being Sir George Julyan, the owner of Rialto. As the latter swept past the stand in the preliminary canter, Sir George looked a little uneasy; so did his companions.

"Is that horse really fit, Julyan?" asked one.

"I should have said emphatically yes on Monday," Julyan replied. "So you notice the difference, eh? Seems short, and inclined to lather. Just my luck if Rialto got a cold on the night of the fire."

Those of the public who knew a horse when they saw one shared the uneasiness. The favourite dropped a point or two in the betting.

As the kaleidoscope of brilliant jackets flashed out in a streaming band from under the eye of the starter Rialto dropped to fourth place, and so continued until at length the horses came into the home stretch.

"Rialto is coming, I see," remarked one of the group behind Gryde.

The latter stole a glance at Sir George's face. The latter was perfectly calm and collected, but his lips flickered like a tongue of flame in a fire.

"I don't think so," he said. "Ribton is riding him."

Just an instant the favourite shot out only to drop back again. Then amidst a perfect babel a rank outsider challenged, Rialto made a desperate effort, and finally was beaten by half a length.

The ring cheered to the echo; everybody else was ominously silent. With a click Sir George snapped his race glasses together.

"Well, they can't say Rialto didn't run a game horse," he said. "Egad, the burning of that bundle or two of straw cost me £40,000."

"Precisely the sum I have won," Gryde told himself. "The pseudo Rialto was a game horse; indeed, a little later on it may be that I have provided Sir George with a better animal than his own. No use staying here any longer. And now we shall see what kind of a turn the real Rialto will do me on Monday."

CHAPTER III

At twenty minutes past three on the following Monday afternoon a ragged-looking colt with a fine turn of speed flashed along between the white posts fencing off thousands of turfites, and once more the ring was rejoicing in the pleasing and remunerative pastime of "skinning the lamb."

Outsiders frequently win big races, but the spectacle of a horse absolutely unknown striding twenty lengths ahead of anything else past the judge's chair is not quite so common. Until the numbers went up, nobody knew who had won the Silverpool.

There was a good deal of raucous mirtn in the ring. But one or two Napoleons of the pencil were observed to look grave. The owner of the fortunate Confetti was supposed to be somewhere on the course, but nobody had seen him.

After the jockey had weighed in, Gunter and "Mr. Smith" discussed the matter calmly.

"You are perfectly satisfied?" asked the latter.

"Well, what do you think?" exclaimed the delighted Gunter. "I've made ten thousand clear. And a prettier plant, a plant more worthy of 'Awley Smart, I never heard tell of. I expect you've done better."

"A trifle," Gryde said drily. "You know what to do next. It seems a pity, but it's the only way to keep the thing from creeping out. Rialto, otherwise Confetti, must never run another race."

Gunter winked knowingly.

"It does seem a pity," he said, "but I'll do exactly as you tell me."

The confederates shook hands and parted. It was the last time they were likely to meet: a piece of information Gryde did not deem it necessary to impart to Gunter. And as the former sat in propria persona and entirely shorn of disguise in his club, he was calmly reading as follows in the special Globe:

THE SILVERPOOL CUP
DEATH OF THE WINNER

The sensational victory of the rank outsider Confetti in the Silverpool Cup to-day is followed by a no less tragic sequel. It appears that whilst the animal was being personally rubbed down by Gunter, his trainer, the colt burst a blood vessel, and died a few minutes later. Confetti had no other engagements this season, but all the same the Duke de Cavour is to be condoled with on his loss.

Gryde smiled as he lay back smoking a thoughtful cigar.

"Really," he told himself, "this has been a very pretty piece of business. And they say there cannot be anything new in the way of a racing fraud. Not only have I proved the contrary, but also I have hit upon a scheme which will never be found out. First I find a horse so like Rialto that I exchange one for the other without fear of detection. Even the Grand Clarendon defect is naturally accounted for. I make a pile of money laying against Rialto—a certainty this. Then the real Rialto, artistically faked, runs as Confetti. This means still more money. And as the Duke is safely out of the way, where he is likely to see no English papers, with friends who don't know a horse from a halter, that avenue of detection is closed. The rest of my money I can safely draw on Monday, and then "Mr. Smith's" place will know him no more. A pity to destroy Rialto, but it was necessary. The course taken renders everything absolutely safe.

"And as to Sackville Mayne? Well, Mr. Mayne is not likely to open his mouth. He has had a thousand pounds for his horse, knowing perfectly well that some swindle was afloat, and though he may wonder, the last thing he will do will be to ask questions. You can always, buy that class of man. Perhaps I ought to have had Bar Sinister, now passing as Rialto, poisoned, but that is a mere detail. And how easy it has all been! Really, next time I must try something with an element of danger in it. Wonder if there is anyone in the billiard-room. I should like a bit of excitement after this humdrum business."

THE "MORRISON RAID" INDEMNITY

CHAPTER I

The Daily Telephone of June 19th last contained the following announcement:

"The claim made by the Randstrand Republic against the Cape Federation Company has at length been settled upon terms. The official arbitrators have assessed the damages at one million of pounds, which is ordered to be paid within the next four weeks. Whether this is the final chapter in the romance of the Morrison Raid remains to be seen. If the latest advices from South Africa are to be trusted, this is merely the prologue."

Thousands of interested Englishmen read the paragraph over the matutinal coffee, but none perused it with more interest than Mr. James Greenbaulm, the eminent Cape merchant, in his Fenchurch Street office.

Greenbaulm had not been in England long. He was understood to be one of the most recent of the Cape millionaires, and he had come to this country with the intention of opening a personal branch in London. For the rest, he was in avowed sympathy with the Randstrand Government, and as frankly against England. Open hostility of this kind is only possible in this country — indeed, we rather seem to encourage it.

A large, pursy, clean-shaven man, with sub-Semitic cast of face and piercing grey eyes was Greenbaulm. He was the incarnation of sleek respectability. His very garments suggested Capital. The type can be recognised at a glance; it is met only in the City, though the genus does occasionally stray as far as Manchester and Liverpool.

An electric gleam flashed behind Greenbaulm's spectacles. He laid the Telephone aside with an air of decision; then he quitted his office and made his way to a set of chambers in one of the narrow streets off Cheapside. Hereabouts are situated the offices of Lemesurier and Co., merchants.

Greenbaulm demanded to see the head of the firm, and was at once admitted into the latter's private room. A thin man, with sanguine, eager face and thin nervous lips, rose to greet him. Enthusiast was writ large all over him. There was no bigger crank and no more brilliant specimen of a Little Englander in the House of Commons than Stephen Lemesurier. Some men have creeds, others have nothing but passions. Lemesurier belonged to the latter category.

The Morrison Raid had stirred all the emotion in his nature. He would have given a good round sum to see England driven bag and baggage out of the Randstrand. And if open hostilities broke out, he had publicly announced his intention of giving £100,000 to the oppressed Republic. Neither was Lemesurier alone in this determination. There were others besides himself, as Greenbaulm was perfectly aware.

"You have seen the Telephone?" said the latter. "What are you going to do?"

"Act," Lemesurier cried. "As a Randstrander yourself, you must know as much as I do. There is trouble brewing out yonder; our Government means to force the Republic into fighting—there will be more disgraceful landgrabbing. But this award is a slice of luck I hardly expected."

"We haven't got it yet," Greenbaulm said drily.

"No, but it is certain to come. The question is, will it come in time? I think not. Therefore a few of us have decided to advance the million to the accredited agent of the Randstrand Republic, taking a lien on the award as security. Nine of us are prepared to put down our money at any time; indeed, it is already posted in the United Cape Bank here. We want one more man to find a tenth."

Greenbaulm produced a cheque-book from his pocket and dashed off a draft. This he coolly handed to Lemesurier.

"That matter is settled then," he said. "I take it Dr. Leyden can draw the money at any time he requires. Of course you know that every penny of this is going to be laid out in Brussels."

"For munitions of war. Certainly I do. I quite understood that was the object of the advance. It would never do for the stuff to come from Germany, though Germany is backing up the Republic. But isn't it quite time that Dr. Leyden should reach here from Berlin?"

"Leyden is not in Berlin at all," Greenbaulm explained. "The papers are all wrong. He is in London—or, at least, he will be to-morrow—for a few days, and he will call upon you at a time to be arranged for the cheque."

"I should like to have his address," Lemesurier suggested.

"He has no address. It is better not. He will call upon you the first thing. And you will recommend him— we are strangers—to come and see me at Hammersmith. You can give him directions where to find me. And the sooner this business is settled the better, you understand."

Whereupon Greenbaulm went off about his business. A peculiar smile flickered about the corners of his mouth as he went along.

"If I were an absolute monarch," he muttered, "I would hang a man like that. This is the only country in the world where a man can boast of being a traitor with impunity. But you are going to have an expensive lesson, Mr. Lemesurier."

The inference of all this was perfectly plain. A few fanatics were going to advance the sinews of war to a prospective enemy. And Dr. Leyden, the accredited agent of the opposing State, was coming to fetch the money. In specie, the same could be transferred to the Continent and there exchanged for lethal weapons.

But Greenbaulm did not return immediately to his office; in fact, he was not seen there for the rest of the day. Instead of this he called a cab and astonished the driver by an order to proceed to Poplar. The transaction was agreed to upon terms highly satisfactory to the jehu.*

[* Jehu - cab-driver. After King Jehu in the Old Testament, known for driving his chariot furiously.]

Most people knew, by name at least, the famous Poplar establishment of Elswick and Company. There everything ingenious and mechanical that goes upon wheels is manufactured. Greenbaulm was evidently expected, for one of the partners met him.

"Well, and how are things progressing?" asked the latter.

"Both your commissions are executed," was the reply. "Your suggestion as to the motor-car has proved a brilliant success. There is practically no vibration; we have attained a speed of eighteen miles an hour with comparative ease, and the machine would carry a ton or two into the bargain."

Greenbaulm professed himself to be perfectly satisfied. On a trial the new motor proved to be a perfect success.

"Then you will send that to Hammersmith to-day," he said. "And now can we have a run on the launch? I am more interested in her."

The tiny, graceful steam launch was also Greenbaulm's invention. Steam was the motive power, and oil formed the fuel. The beauty of the arrangement was that one person could work the whole affair.

"But there is one thing I would impress upon you," said the engineer, once the trial trip was over. "A high-pressure engine like this wants constant care. The steam runs up and down in the gauge like quicksilver. Let it but touch this point and you might as well have half a ton of dynamite explode on board."

Greenbaulm smiled, and promised to be careful.

"I shall see to it myself," he said.

"This kind of thing is my pet hobby. In most cases I shall probably go out alone. By the way, you had better let me have this little toy at Hammersmith this week. I shall probably require it on Saturday, and the covered dock is all ready."

Greenbaulm drove from Poplar direct to Hammersmith, and it may be mentioned as worthy of record that one cabman, at least, in London retired to rest that night absolutely content with his fare. Records are always pleasing.

As Greenbaulm fully expected—indeed, he had made his arrangements with an elaborate minuteness and care which might have astonished Lemesurier had he known of them—Dr. Leyden came down to Hammersmith the next evening. The latter arrived in time for dinner. He came without fuss and ceremony—a wiry, leathery-looking man with a keen restless eye. Energy was the dominant note of this character. Greenbaulm was setting down to dinner as he arrived.

In the coolest way possible Leyden shook hands.

"Possibly you have been expecting me?" he suggested.

"I looked forward to you as a certainty," Greenbaulm replied. "I knew you would go to Lemesurier, and that he would give you my message. Far better come here than seek the publicity of an hotel."

Leyden pulled his chair up to the table in a most business-like way. He was the class of man who could have dined comfortably on a powder magazine. He surveyed the perfectly appointed dining table with calm satisfaction. Every well-balanced man prefers a good dinner to a bad one.

"Try this sole," Greenbaulm suggested, "it is one of my cook's inspirations. Your interview with Lemesurier was perfectly satisfactory?"

"Quite. I have the cheque for the million in my pocket. I had no idea we had so many good friends in England."

"Lemesurier is a fanatic and a fool," Greenbaulm said calmly. "As for the rest of them, there is precious little philanthropy about the business. They are merely fostering us for speculative purposes. It will cost £100,000 each, and cheap at the price."

Leyden's eyes flashed.

"You believe we shall be defeated?' he demanded. "You are of opinion that the Randstrand will become an English possession?"

"I am a patriot like yourself," said Greenbaulm. "What are your plans?"

"My plans are fairly simple. To-morrow afternoon I proceed with my secretary, Ernst, whom I have left in London, to get this money. Without declaring the same, we shall ship it from Queenborough for Rotterdam. Once in Belgium we shall change it for munitions of war. I may go to Berlin."

"There is no occasion to do that," Greenbaulm interrupted. "At the present moment, strictly incognito, the Emperor is in Brussels."

Leyden expressed his astonishment. That the Emperor in question had a strong sympathy with the Randstrand movement, he knew perfectly well. And Greenbaulm proceeded to give chapter and verse for his statement in such a manner as to put all further doubt out of the question.

"There is some startling development on foot," Greenbaulm concluded, "though I cannot be any more definite. I can tell you this—the Emperor may send for you at any moment, when you will have to go at once. By this time his Majesty knows perfectly well you are here."

Anything further Greenbaulm declined to say. Indeed, it was not his cue to be any more definite in the matter. He intended to convey to Leyden that he knew all the weighty secret, and he succeeded admirably.

"His Majesty is, to put it mildly, erratic," said the latter. "He means well, but I am terribly afraid of that impulsiveness of his. All I hope is that he won't send for me till I can get the money under way."

Greenbaulm rose from the table.

"Meanwhile we will discuss this business no further," he said. "If you have had sufficient wine, perhaps you will smoke a cigar. I have some excellent ones here which I can fully recommend."

"I confess a good cigar has its points," Leyden smiled.

Greenbaulm proceeded to open a cupboard in the wall, from which he took a large cedar box. Something clanked and rattled in the cupboard as he moved. There was a glimpse of blue and gold lace.

Leyden looked curiously at his host.

"You have been a soldier," he said tentatively.

"I have been many things in my time," he said, "and nothing long. But there is one thing I have never been."

"And what is that?" Leyden asked. Greenbaulm's eyes twinkled behind his cigar.

"Found out," he said drily. "And I don't think I ever shall be."

CHAPTER II

Leyden was killing time after breakfast the following morning. There were one or two things to interest him, conspicuous amongst them being the new motor-car, with which, as a great traveller, he was specially delighted; but it may seem a little strange that Greenbaulm said nothing relating to the steam launch now lying snug in the covered dock at the end of the garden. Greenbaulm left his guest in the road busily engaged with the motor.

"Stay as long as you like," he said hospitably. "I must be off to the City. Call in this afternoon and let me know how you get on. I have to dress."

With which Greenbaulm returned to the house. A minute later he hailed Leyden from the gate right down the road.

"A visitor to see you," he said; "come at once."

Leyden made his way as swiftly as possible to the drawing-room. An instant before Greenbaulm was in the dining-room. He made a dart for the cupboard where he had found the cigars on the previous evening; his arms and legs seemed to work like flashes of light, and in less time than it takes to tell,

Greenbaulm was transposed into a military-looking with eye-glass and heavy moustache complete. He literally dived for the cupboard, some door gave way and closed again with a spring, and Greenbaulm was in the drawing-room beyond before Leyden had time to enter the apartment. Fregoli could have done no better.

"You are Dr. Leyden," said the attaché imperiously. "I am Count André."

"The Emperor's private secretary?" said Leyden in his turn.

"The same. I have travelled from Brussels—from Brussels, you understand —post-haste to see you. I have a letter to you from my master. You will be pleased to read it and act on the instructions contained therein without delay."

The letter was passed across the table. Leyden recognised the Imperial hand. Inside the envelope was an address, and an imperious line or two commanding Leyden to repair to the address given without an instant's delay.

"Well," said the attaché" impatiently, "well?."

"I obey," Leyden replied. "I have to see my secretary first, and then anything else goes to the wall. If you will be so good—"

But Count André had already departed. As a matter of fact, seeing the coast was clear he flashed up the stairs.

A minute or two later Greenbaulm, correctly attired, came leisurely into the hall.

"Your friend has gone already?" he asked carelessly.

"My friend would be none the worse for a few lessons in manners," Leyden muttered. "The Emperor desires to see me at once."

"Ah! Then you are summoned to Brussels, after all?"

Leyden explained fully. He also begged Greenbaulm to show him a way out of the difficulty.

"I shall certain to be away for a few days," he said; "and meanwhile you see the necessity for getting that money out of the bank and stowing it safely somewhere." Greenbaulm knitted his brows in thought. Then his face cleared.

"I can see a way out of the difficulty," he said. "See your secretary, in whom you say you have the most implicit confidence; let him come to my office in bank hours, and I will go with him to get the specie we have arranged for. I have a safe here big enough for the Bank of England."

"But we should want a procession of cabs to bring all that bulk here."

"Under ordinary circumstances we might. But as it so happens, my motor-car will come in splendidly. It would be folly, in any case, to leave the money where it is. Would you like to see the safe?"

Leyden expressed his desire to do so. At the end of a passage Greenbaulm opened a door leading into a veritable strong-room. Dark as it was, the place appeared to be perfectly ventilated. Greenbaulm switched on the electric light.

"There," he said, with some little pride, "what do you think of that?"

"Capital!" Leyden cried, catching some of his host's enthusiasm ; "and could not be better. You have got me out of a great difficulty. I'll get up to town as quickly as possible and see Ernst. You will have everything ready at your office by two o'clock—and many thanks for all your kindness."

Greenbaulm saw his visitor safely away, and then returned to the safe. He pulled out one or two of the drawers as if to satisfy himself that all was secure; then, with an inscrutable smile on his face, he ordered out his motor-car, and proceeded alone to steer himself to London.

A little after two and Ernst arrived. Greenbaulm surveyed the latter's magnificent thews and sinews in a dreamy, admiring way.

"I am pleased to see you," he said.

"If you are ready we will proceed to the bank. I trust you will be my guest for the present: you are big enough to see that I don't run off with the million."

The business was transacted at length, and the heavy cases transferred to the motor-car. Weighty as they were, the compact little machine made nothing of them. Then the motor was turned in the direction of Hammersmith

"I am going to take a holiday this afternoon," Greenbaulm explained. "You will want somebody to help you to get those cases into the safe. Once there, I shall make you a present of the key till they are removed."

The work took some considerable time, and at length was accomplished, the cases all being piled up in one corner of the safe. Ernst was loud in his praises over the strength and compactness of the strong-room.

"And even now you have not seen all its resources," Greenbaulm explained.

"Look here." He pulled down a flap and disclosed a cupboard. It was stored with plates and glasses, a corkscrew, a can-opener, and any quantity of preserved provisions. Besides these, there were wines and spirits in liberal quantities.

"What does all this mean?" asked the amazed Ernst.

"It is a fad of mine," Greenbaulm replied. "I was once accidentally locked in a safe for a day, and I have a horror of it since. You see this door closes with a spring there—don't be afraid, I have the key in my pocket. That bread was put in here this morning in case of accidents. Try that flap below the door."

Ernst crossed the floor to gratify his curiosity; as he did so Greenbaulm stood upon the pile of bullion boxes and touched a nob on the roof. There was a clang and a rattle, half the floor fell away sideways, shooting out the treasure and Greenbaulm into space, and closing again, absolutely displaying no joint before Ernst could turn round.

He rubbed his eyes in astonishment. He was absolutely alone. It seemed like an evil dream. Then it flashed across Ernst that he was trapped. The cupboard behind the door had disclosed nothing but a letter addressed to the captive.

"You will be left here for two or three days," it ran. "It is not the slightest use to make any noise, because nobody can possibly hear you. There are plenty of provisions here, and in due course the key of this safe will be forwarded to Dr. Leyden with an explanatory letter. There is also an extensive collection of literature behind the bottles in the cupboard."

Ernst dashed the letter furiously to the ground.

"Tricked and swindled!" he groaned. "What will the Doctor say?"

Meanwhile, the pseudo Greenbaulm, alias Felix Gryde, was anything but idle. All his plans were complete, down to the minutest detail. Neither was there anybody to interfere with him in the house, for every servant in the place had been got rid of under one pretext or another. As to the premises, they would not be required by Gryde after to-day.

The ingenious safe had been made to his own plans, and the whole thing arranged as soon as the aggrandisement of the Randstrand million was decided upon. Gryde found himself outside the safe upon an incline plane, down which the boxes of specie were shot into a wheel-barrow ready for the purpose. One by one they were transferred to the steam launch.

With the precious burden aboard, and Gryde alone besides, the arrow-like craft shot down the river. At the end of an hour she fetched up alongside a yacht evidently awaiting her advent. But the individual who looked up from the liliput engine-room did not appear to be Gryde at all, but a greasy mechanic. It was Gryde all the same.

"Hullo, there," he said gruffly, but with a nasal twang, "guess I've brought that machinery for your governor. You're to drop down to the Point and wait for the boss. He calculates to be aboard you at five."

The bullion, or machinery, as Gryde called it, was slung over the side of the Osprey and dumped unceremoniously into the hold. Then Gryde put about, and swung up the river again. By this time he had destroyed his last disguise. For the nonce he was Greenbaulm again. Several boating parties who lived in the vicinity recognised the capitalist.

Gryde's eyes were flashing like stars. He passed down the stairs and into the stuffy engine-room. The steam was particularly high in the gauge. Heedless of this fact, and heedless of the engineer's instructions, he stirred the fire. The man's nerve must have been of iron.

"I must not delay longer," he muttered. Once on deck again, he lashed the rudder, steering in a straight line down stream. Nothing could happen for at least five minues. Then, taking care that he was not observed, Greenbaulm dived into the water. He did not come to the surface till the bank was reached, and the bank just there formed a portion of his own grounds.

"Let her go if she likes now," he said, "so far as I—"

Crash! A noise like the clang of ten thousand hammers, the shrill scream of escaping steam. Then, as if torn apart by some marvellous unseen force, the steam launch burst, threw up its bows and disappeared.

"A dramatic exit," Gryde said with a sardonic smile.

He lingered long enough to see a score of boats proceed to the scene of the accident, and for a crowd of spectators to gather on the opposite bank. After that he proceeded to the now deserted house, and a little while later a typical Yankee of the better and smarter type hailed a cabman close by.

"Look here," he said, "you've got to take me to the Point. My yacht's waiting for me there, and I don't want to miss this tide."

Arrived at the Point, "Colonel Barber" was rowed out to the Osprey, and almost before the latest Thames catastrophe was sent flashing Fleet Street way, the yacht was dropping out wiih the tide. Gryde went below without even taking the trouble to ask after his precious cargo.

It was a clear starlight night, soft and balmy, and lying outside St. Malo, Gryde was seated comfortably in his cabin reading the sequel to the story of the Morrison Raid Indemnity. A fortnight had passed since that little incident, and meanwhile, at one port and another, "Colonel Gunter" had parted with most of his cases of "machinery." It was in the Star that the story briefly appeared:

"The outlines of a startling story reach us as we go to press. It concerns the Morrison Indemnity, but we cannot say much more at present. What we hear is startling enough in all conscience. A stolen million, the secretary to a Randstrand celebrity imprisoned in a safe provisioned for the purpose, and the whole fraud planned by a millionaire whose name is not unlike Greenbaulm.

"To crown the thing the money has disappeared, and so has the pseudo millionaire, beyond all question killed by an explosion on his own steam launch. Some highly sensational details are expected, for Secretary Ernst has not been too discreet since his release, and we shall spare no pains to get to the root of matters."

Gryde smiled as he lay back in his deck chair. He could afford to puff his choice cigar with perfect equanimity.

"I don't suppose they will spare any pains," he muttered, "but they can't succeed. Neither will the true facts ever be made public," a prophecy which up to now has been fulfilled to the letter.

That sensational number of the Star has yet to appear.

CLEOPATRA'S ROBE

"I wish," said Cora Coventry, "I wish that I was the Queen!"

The solitary listener laughed softly. There was a shaded lamp at Cora's pearly elbow, the red drawn silk of which caused the riband across the man's breast to look like blood. As to the rest of the room, it was luxury in shadowland, refinement implied rather than accentuated. Cora Coventry was a tangle of fascinating mysteries. Not the least remarkable of these was whence came her exquisite taste. Perhaps those liquid black eyes were formed for colour, and Cora had commenced life in unmentionable purlieus.

As to the rest, it is not wise, perhaps, to inquire too closely. On the score of finance Lord Lyndon could have spoken with authority had he chosen to do so. Lyndon was rich, a diplomat, and a speaker of parts. Also he was popularly supposed to hold the first place in Cora's affections. The luxury was a costly one, but the friendship of the most fascinating woman in London is not to be obtained by constancy and five farthings.

Lyndon shot a jet of blue smoke in parallel lines from each arched nostril. He lounged back with the narrowed eyes of a connoisseur. Cora was always a picture to him. He liked expensive drawings of this kind.

"What do you want to be a queen for?" he asked.

"Only for this year. Lovely things are a passion with me, you know. And this is the sixtieth year of—O! just try and imagine the presents! I could commit a dozen murders to call them mine."

"I had no idea you had such feelings. Cora, is it possible that you have a heart concealed about you somewhere?"

"Perhaps. There used to be a man I knew once—I have not seen him for years—"

"Cora in love! A new sensation. Tell me all about it."

Cora laughed. The dragon's blood of the lampshade crept into her cheeks.

"I shall do nothing of the kind," she said. "I may never see him again. He could do with me what he pleased. O! he was a man!"

"Which means to imply, Cora?"

"What you will. When are you going to take me to see those presents? What of that wonderful robe that everybody is talking about—Cleopatra's Robe?"

"It isn't there. As you are aware, the same was a present from the Sultan in honour of the Diamond Jubilee, forwarded by a special retinue and all the rest of it. Under existing circumstances a certain gracious Lady declines to receive the gift. Without unnecessary fuss, the offering has been declined, and there is an end of it. Abdul Agiz has still hopes, however."

"Abdul Agiz is the favourite entrusted with the robe?"

"Precisely. His position is what diplomats would call a delicate one. If he goes home without accomplishing his mission he will probably find himself in a permanent berth on the Bosphorus. And he is bound to fail."

Cora followed with the deepest interest. Things rare and beautiful had a wonderful fascination for her. And of all the fabrics in the universe none had a stranger history than the robe, or rather shawl, in question.

Beyond all question the marvellous piece of workmanship had belonged to Cleopatra. Antony might have languished in its brilliant folds. Not a stitch of the remarkable blend of colours had lost a shade in tone. It was of cobweb delicacy with the strength of pliant steel, a woven picture old as the hills. And for all anyone knew to the contrary, the secret of manufacture lay under the Pyramids.

There had been war over those few yards of loomed hair and colour. For generations it had lain hidden in the treasure house at Teheran. Then by some stratagem it had passed into the possession of Turkey, where it had remained ever since. This unique possession had now been refused by a sovereign who looked coldly upon massacre and declined to recognise crime as a regal virtue.

This history Lyndon gave with the enthusiasm of the virtuoso. Cora listened with a pang of regret. She would have liked to have seen this thing, but it was too late now. She laid her hand upon the bell.

"I believe you are telling me this to annoy me," she said. "I am going to turn you out as a punishment. Go away."

Lyndon retired. He had studied the lovely and costly picture quite enough for one night. Satiety in beauty and tobacco alike cloys the palate. Hardly had he gone when there came the pulsation of the front door bell.

"I can't see him, whoever he is," Cora told her maid.

But it was too late. The intruder was already in the room.

"You will see me," he said coolly. "Send that woman away."

"Yes, go away," Cora said in a curiously choked voice. "So it is you Paul."

The man so addressed smiled. He sank into the padded recesses of a chair with the air of one who is absolutely at home. He had a handsome, almost boyish, face—his blue eyes seemed to glitter with magnetic fire. For the present, he elected to be known as Paul Chaffers. His real name was Felix Gryde.

"You are pleased to see me, Cora?" he said.

"I am always pleased to see you," Cora responded in the same hoarse tones, "passionately pleased. And yet I am frightened also. Why do you frighten me?"

"Because I am your master, I suppose. Really, Cora, we are two wonderful people. Together we might do anything."

"Then why don't we stay together and do it?"

"Because it is the one golden rule of my life never to trust anyone but myself. Still, you are going to help me now, and I am going to help you, and you are going to be paid £10,000 for your trouble, Cora."

"What is the last piece of masterly audacity?"

"I will tell you. Everybody has heard of that wonderful Cleopatra shawl which the Sultan sent over here only to be refused. I am going to annex it."

Cora laughed. There was nothing mocking about her mirth. She was merely amused, and indeed pleased, at the audacity of the suggestion. She knew enough of Gryde to feel certain that he would succeed in his undertaking. She was absolutely in the power of this man, the man of whom she knew nothing. She did not even credit his assertion that Paul Chaffers was his real name. He came and went when he liked; of his aims and pursuits she was hopelessly ignorant. And now, after the lapse of months, he returned, masterful, assured as ever.

"That is a strange thing," she said. "I would give an eye to possess it myself."

"But the thing is absolutely impossible for you."

"And not for you. And yet I am to be your tool in the matter."

"At the rate of some £3,000 per hour, which is a fancy price, Cora. The Persian Government would pay anything in reason for that glorified rag, and so far as I am concerned, the matter is a purely commercial transaction."

"And I am going to pull the chestnut out of the fire."

"Not so as to burn your fingers, beautiful one. Come, Cora, when I say a thing, you know it has to be done."

Cora nodded. A fluttering sigh escaped from her red lips.

"Very well," she said, as if speaking against her will. "Tell me your plans."

"Presently. You asked me just now where I had been lately. For some months I have been located in Pera and Adrianople. I have been learning weaving—look at this."

So saying, Gryde took from his waistcoat pocket a small square of fabric folded many times. With a dexterous movement he shot out his hand, and then, as if by magic, the casket was covered with yards of some exquisitely beautiful material. Cora pounced upon it with a cry of wild delight.

"O, is it not marvellous?" she almost screamed. "Did anyone ever see such exquisite colours and such blending of shades? Look at me, Paul."

She caught up the diaphanous folds of spun daylight and twisted them about her graceful form. The Serpent of Old Nile herself was not more fascinating.

"Paul," she cried, "you wonderful man! This is the Robe of Cleopatra."

"No," Gryde replied, "merely a facsimile of the same. A remarkable old Syrian at Pera told me that. Goodness knows it cost trouble and money enough to get it. That unique weaver has actually repaired the real article (he said one of his ancestors from whom he got the secret actually made it), and he surreptitiously copied the pattern. But for the historic value, one is quite as precious as the other."

"Imprisoned sunshine," said Cora. "Is—is this for me?"

Gryde shook his head with a smile.

"O, no," he said, "that is part of the cosmic scheme. I did not dwell qua Mussulman in one of the dirtiest dens in Europe for weeks to spoil everything by an act of foolish good nature. You are going to the Covent Garden fancy dress ball on Thursday?"

Cora nodded. This sudden change of conversation did not surprise her. And all the time she kept her hold upon the dazzling fabric as if loth to part with it.

"You can keep that till Thursday night if you like!" said Gryde, who seemed to read Cora's mind like an open book, "and when the evening comes you are to take it along, properly hidden. I will give you full instructions when the time comes. To-morrow night you are going to entertain myself and a friend to dinner."

"As you will. I have another engagement, which I will put off. And who may be your victim?— I mean friend — who is coming here?"

Gryde rose and lighted a cigarette. The ghost of a smile flickered about his lips. Cora liked to see him smile; it was, she said, the only assurance she had that he was human.

"The name," she repeated imperiously, "the name?"

"Abdul Agiz," Gryde said drily. "Good-night, fair charmer."

CHAPTER II

The weakest part of a man's armour is the strongest, otherwise ordinary mortals would lack the gratifying knowledge that even great men are guilty of doing foolish things. Without doubt Prince Abdul Agiz was one of the astutest subjects of the Ruler of Turkey, but Gryde, who had already formed his acquaintance, had discovered the weak. spot and laid his plans accordingly.

The poetic vein in Abdul Agiz' nature rendered him extremely susceptible where the fair sex were concerned. On a previous occasion he had enjoyed the advantage of a two years' residence in England, so that he was no stranger to our language and customs. Nor had he been here on his present mission long before Cora Coventry had caught his critical eye. And when Gryde offered an introduction, he accepted the offer eagerly.

The evening appointed, Gryde called round at the hotel for his friend. Several times already had he been in the Prince's private room. He knew where the precious robe lay concealed and how jealously it was guarded by Abdul Agiz' suite. The latter received Gryde with effusion.

"You promised to tell me something about a certain charming lady," he said.

"O, yes—about Mrs. Coventry. She is not a widow, as you seem to imagine. Her husband is a distinguished Oriental scholar and diplomatist who is now on his way home from the East; indeed, he may arrive at any time. Next week I could hardly have promised you the privilege I have managed to secure for you to-night."

"Then the lady probably is acquainted with the East as well."

"By no means," Gryde replied. "For some reason or another she detests all mention of it. And yet, strange to say, her favourite servant is a Persian with only a limited knowledge of English. You may get a chance to converse with her. There she is."

By this time the cab had been dismissed, and Gryde and his companion were standing amongst the flowers and ferns in Cora Coventry's vestibule. At the same moment a typical Eastern figure crossed the floor and disappeared.

"It makes one feel quite homely," Abdul Agiz muttered.

In the dimly-lighted drawing-room Cora received them. Abdul was conscious of some white dazzling dream floating around a pair of great liquid eyes that seemed to set him gasping and helpless for the time. Cora took possession of his soul and played with it like a toy. Gryde said little—his chair was a stall, he was watching a play of his own writing. This snake and bird business pleased him.

Then they went into dinner. It is, perhaps, sufficient to say that when Abdul was pressed to take wine he did so. Subsequently he had no recollection of doing anything of the kind. It was all part of the same poetic dream.

Cora rose at length. Abdul's dark eyes followed her rapturously. He remained in a kind of daze, till Gryde suggested a move to the drawing-room. Here cigarettes and coffee after Abdul's own heart awaited them. There was only one crease in the glorious roseleaf; it seemed to the Oriental that Gryde was superfluous.

Almost before Abdul could formulate this thought a servant entered bearing upon a tray a telegram, which he handed to Gryde. The latter read with a gesture of annoyance.

"I am afraid I shall have to leave you," he said. "My message is most peremptory."

Figments of the condemnatory side of the Koran came to Abdul's lips. Then he lolled in the lap of Paradise again as Cora bade him stay. Why should he go because Gryde was called away? she asked. Gryde echoed the sentiment.

Then followed the most dreamy, delightful hour Abdul Agiz had ever passed in his life. He made no attempt to stem the stream of fascination; on the contrary, he lay down and allowed it to flow over him.

Cora put forth all her powers. Her claims were silken; but then beauty leads us by a single hair. Abdul never quite realised himself till he felt the cool night breeze on his face as he turned homeward.

He had promised to do something. What was it? The dream began to slowly disentangle itself from its rosy intricate folds. How wonderfully seductive the music had been! What marvellous eyes Cora had!

O, yes, Abdul had it at last. He promised to aid and abet Cora in a delightful escapade. She was going alone and incognito on Thursday to a fancy dress ball at Covent Garden. Abdul had received minute instructions as to what she was going to wear. She would go unmasked, and then—

A look from the luminous eyes filled the hiatus. Would Abdul try and be there? Might dogs defile the grave of his revered grandmother if he failed. To put it plainly, no lunatic on the right side of Bedlam was ever more helplessly lost in love than Abdul at that moment. There was a lightness in his head, a strange elasticity of limb. The stars seem to bend and whisper of Cora to him. A day with her was worth a cycle of Cathay—or any other place for the matter of that. Constantinople and the Sultan's wrath, the doom of failure receded in the roseate mist.

"Will I not be there!" Abdul murmured. "Will I not! Surely such a creature never drew the breath of life... and I am not without experience. To kiss those lips... I suppose they have been kissed. Who knows but what I—but that is nonsense. I exist merely till Thursday—till then a clod, a vegetable."

All of which goes to prove that Abdul Agiz was very far gone indeed.

A thousand lamps shone o'er fair women and brave men. Very seldom had Covent Garden presented a more brilliant and attractive appearance—a trifle shoddy, perhaps, if analysed, but it does not do to be hypercritical in such matters.

Nathless, the band was perfection, a great proportion of the dresses striking and original. Well-known faces looked from the boxes, a few society people on the floor leavened the lump. Half in shadow, a tall, graceful figure in black, with startling white splashes on her dress, stood as if waiting for someone. Her features were partially concealed in a lace shawl. A vivid smile gave expression to the scarlet lips.

Presently there passed by her a slightly almond-eyed foreigner. He, too, seemed on the look-out for someone. He started as he saw the magpie figure. Despite his outward calm he thrilled to his finger tips.

"You?" he whispered, tentatively.

Cora laughed. With a caressing gesture she slipped her fingers under Abdul's arm.

"I thought you had forsaken me," she whispered. "Shall we dance?"

But, alas! in this respect Abdul's education had been neglected. Still, so long as Cora graciously inclined to palmy seclusion and tender confidence, it mattered little. Abdul was annoyed presently to find it supper-time. He begged for another few minutes, but Cora was obdurate.

"I am mortal," she said, flashing her teeth in a brilliant smile, "and you are insatiable. Come! I will give you a little time afterwards, and perhaps—"

Abdul understood, or thought he did, which came to the same thing. The honied treasure of the scarlet lips might yet be his. As for the supper, it was a mere frittering away of golden moments. Cora chattered idly, Abdul listening.

"Is not this delightful?" she said. "Gather your- Ah!"

The words seemed to be frozen on her lips, her eyes filled with terror. Some person or thing there seemed to fascinate Cora.

"What is it?" Abdul asked.

"Ah! You see that man, the big man with the stern face supping alone by the side of that oleander, yonder? Don't stare, look."

"I see the man. Why should you be afraid of him?"

"For the best of all possible reasons. He is my husband."

Abdul started. The climax bid fair to be a dramatic one.

"Your husband has returned unexpectedly," he said lamely.

"O, yes. That is one of his virtues, you understand. If Jasper was to discover I had visited a place like this alone he would kill me. And yet he must suspect something. You cannot possibly imagine how jealous he is. And he knows this dress."

"We can escape by yonder door. Then I could get you a conveyance of—"

"And perhaps meet one of his spies in the entrance. One never knows. Jealousy amounts to a disease with my husband. But we must get out of this."

Trembling in every limb, Cora rose and hurried from the supper room, Abdul following. A brief backward glance proved the fact that the jealous one had noticed nothing. In a secluded corner, the darker for the contrast with the brilliant arcs beyond, Cora sat shivering.

"What can I do for you?" Abdul asked.

"Hush!" Cora replied sharply, "I am thinking. I begin to see a way. You have a servant somewhere. I know you never go far without one."

"My faithful Assan is even now down in the portico."

"Then bring him up at once. There will be no attempt made to prevent you, and then I can show you a way to save me. Go!"

Abdul turned away. He came back presently, Assan following behind.

"I am going to send your servant for a disguise," Cora explained, "only he understands no English and I can write no Turkish. Is it not providential that you can do it for me? You have a pencil and tablet? Good! Now write."

Cora proceeded to dictate as follows:

"There is a plot on foot to deprive me of my most valued possession. You understand. Ask no questions, but give bearer the case at once. It is on the second shelf in the safe in my room. I shall be with you as soon as I can."

"That is all?" Abdul asked.

"It is quite sufficient," Cora said significantly. "Had I not you to do this for me I know not what might have happened. Give me the paper, quick!"

She snatched it from Abdul's hands and placed it in those of the messenger. Then she bent and whispered a word or two in the latter's ear in his own language. They were all the Turkish she knew, but they had been carefully rehearsed

"To jour master's hotel, to Ben Ali at once," she said. "Go, slave!"

Abdul did not catch the words. He did not seek to detain his servant, but suffered him to go instanter. He was to return to the same spot.

"You are no longer frightened?" Abdul asked.

"Not now. You understand that I see my way clear. My husband may deem me to be here, but when my disguise comes I could pass him boldly if I saw him searching for me as I passed. And but for you, there would have been no escape."

"What are you going to give me for a reward?" Abdul asked.

Cora held her head back with a caressing smile. Three-quarters of an hour had passed, and it was high time the messenger returned. Then Cora's eyes lighted as she detected Assan threading his way through the glittering kaleidoscope.

"We are a commercial people," she said, "and pay by results. You can send in your bill, and then—call for payment. Ah, here he is!"

Assan came forward, carrying a flat, shabby-looking case in his hand. Cora snatched the case from the messenger and bade him begone. A minute later the case was open, and the tiny recess filled with yards of some wonderful diaphanous fabric.

"This is not mine," Cora cried. "What has the fool done?"

Abdul was not slow to grasp the mystery.

"I know," he said, in thick, agitated tones. "He made a mistake; he did not understand the address from you. He took the letter written by me to my subordinate, and the latter has sent me—Cleopatra's Robe. After all, the mistake was a natural one. Give it me; give it up at once, I say."

Cora laughed defiantly. She had already wound the priceless stuff around her in sinuous folds like that of a snake.

"I will not," she said. "Touch me and I will bring the hoard down upon you. You dare to threaten me when my very life, my reputation, is in danger!"

"But my master, the Sultan!"

"A fig for your master. O, I know what this is—I read the papers. Personally, I would not give a penny a yard for it. All the same, it is going to keep me safe till I reach the portico. You fool, follow me and all will be well."

Abdul followed hopelessly. Like a flash of light, Cora made her way to the portico.

"Call me a cab," she said to Abdul; "then take one yourself, and drive off first. Tell the man to put you down by the corner near my house. I will do the same, and then I will return your gaudy rag. Give me the case."

Abdul obeyed. The next twenty minutes were singularly unhappy ones He would have been more unhappy still could he have been in the same cab with Cora and watched her movements.

First of all she took from the bosom of her dress the facsimile of the Cleopatra Robe as supplied to her by Gryde. This she proceeded to place in the case. Then the real treasure was folded up and securely hidden where the copy had come from. When Abdul joined Cora she handed the box to him with a smile.

"There!" she said, "nothing to make such a fuss about, after all. I have to thank you for a perfect disguise, despite yourself. And I shall be obliged if you will open the box under this lamp, and make sure I have not robbed you."

One glance satisfied Abdul. When he looked up again Cora was a fleeting shadow.

"Stop!" he cried. "When shall I see you again? I cannot—"

But the dull bang of a street-door was the one chilly response.

"There!" Cora was remarking a little later, as she sat opposite Gryde. "Who shall say I have not fulfilled your instructions to the letter? You have that priceless relic, and Abdul has gone off quite easy in his mind. If it is found out?"

"It will not be found out," Gryde said calmly. "The imitation is too marvellous for anyone but an expert. Abdul will return home to be bowstrung in consequence of the failure of his mission, and the robe will be placed in the treasury for perhaps the next century to come. And, after all, the trick was a very simple one."

"But the triumph of the Persian Government in the recovery of—"

"There will be no triumph. The Oriental nature is not like ours. The mere possession of the thing will suffice, without boasting of it. There is a deal of miserly secretiveness in your Eastern type of man."

"You will make a deal of money out of it?" Cora asked.

"About half a million," Gryde responded, "unless those people save unnecessary trouble by cutting my throat as a settlement in full. But they will find me quite prepared for that kind of thing."

"You are a wonderful man," Cora said, admiringly.

Gryde smiled as he rose to go.

"Really I am," he said. "And now I must take myself off, for fear of coming in contact with the jealous husband. Good-night, Cora!"

"Good-night! But I shall see you again to-morrow?"

"I fear not," said Gryde. "I start early on my way for Teheran. But before I go I shall not fail to send you your share of the plunder."

THE ROSY CROSS

CHAPTER I

Job Potter cannot by any stretch of imagination be called a euphonious name, but in the case of a capitalist a little thing like this is excusable. Between Potter the millionaire and the Hon. Augustus Vansittart, the dude, the gulf was a wide one. There were, however, reasons for the friendship between them.

A common-looking little man was Potter, but shrewd withal. There was nothing solid to be obtained from Vansittart. Only there was a Mrs. Potter, away in England, ambitious for social distinction, and Vansittart might be used as a lever. Vansittart was quite ready to respond. The dinners given by Potter at the Royal Banner, Chicago, were quite poems in their way. They were dining together this evening.

"This," Potter remarked, "is my last business trip to America. A couple of months more and I return home to settle down."

"Ditto," responded the exquisite Augustus. "I haven't seen my people since I was a lad. They—er—sent me over here. And now I've come into money, don't you know. Accounts for my being here. Gad, it's worth something to have a Bond Street coat on again. All the same, the Bishop is a nuisance."

"What Bishop?" Potter asked interestedly.

"His Grace of Croydon. Sort of connection. Came out here for his health. So I arranged to meet 'em here and go home together. They arrive to-morrow. Guess they won't recognise me. And it's a good job Lady Ella's along."

"And who may Lady Ella be?"

Potter rang the title sonorously.

"Niece, old chap. Regular beauty, and a flier. But don't worry. I shall certainly tell them how kind you have been to me, and if you like, when they do come, I'll get the old man and Ella to come and dine with you."

Potter beamed. If he played his cards right, here was a fine opening for the introduction to capital S Society for which Mrs. Potter yearned. More for an advertisement of this kind than anything else, he had bought the "Rosy Cross" diamond.

"Delighted," he said. "I'll show Lady Ella the 'Rosy Cross.' Women love diamonds. Suppose you saw by the papers I'd bought the stone?"

Vansittart succumbed to a yawn.

"Yes," he drawled; "you syndicate chaps will be after the earth next."

"It's a pretty stone," Potter said parenthetically. "Like to see it?"

Vansittart nodded, but did not enthuse, although the famous gem known as the "Rosy Cross" was exciting a deal of interest just at present. The stone, or rather a cluster of stones, long and twisted like a snake, was supposed to have been found in California, but good judges declared it to be a stolen Brazilian treasure brought to that favoured spot, buried and dug up again so as to give the yarn local colour.

Roughly speaking, the stones might have been worth £100,000—as a matter of fact, they might have fetched double that. Potter brought the curio from his adjacent bedroom, for they were dining privately, and handed it to Vansittart.

"Pretty little thing, isn't it?" he asked complacently.

Vansittart boiled up enough enthusiasm to say yes. Had Potter only known how near he stood to being shot in cold blood and robbed of his treasure then and there, he would have looked less satisfied. Vansittart, otherwise Felix Gryde, lighted another cigarette with the air of a man who regards life as too violent an exercise.

"Put the thing up," he said. "Think I'll go to bed; I'm tired to death. Let you know when the Bishop and Lady Ella come along."

Three days later Potter was flustered and delighted to hear that the Right Reverend the Bishop of Croydon had arrived with Lady Ella, and would the millionaire mind if they dined with him on the Friday? Their eastern train left on the Monday morning, so there was not much time.

It need hardly be said that Potter was delighted. The manager of the Royal Banner was interviewed, and departed with carte blanche and a promise of no quibbling over the bill if everything was "done up to the 'ilt."

Thereupon a suite of rooms were actually transformed for the occasion. A bed-chamber was specially furnished for Lady Ella, also a dressing-room for the Bishop, to say nothing of a drawing-room where after the amber wine had ceased to foam her ladyship should dazzle the men with her beauty and dispense to them coffee and sweet smiles.

"Blow the expense," said Potter; "these are the nobs I'm after. I'll give these toffs something to talk about when they get home. Lord, won't Maria be pleased when she hears all about it!"

The appointed time came and with it Lady Ella and the Bishop. They were gracious and pleasant to the last degree. Before the evening was over Potter felt that Lady Ella had no equal in the wide world. A woman so beautiful and so fascinating had never before crossed his limited horizon.

She was elusive as a dream and fascinating as Ninon. An instinctive knowledge of the genuine was amongst Potter's many gifts—an expert in precious stones is born, not made—and he knew that Lady Ella rang true. Without any previous knowledge of patrician dames, he would at once have recognised and resented any attempt to pass off a counterfeit article.

Lady Ella was gracious and friendly. She appeared to recognise Potter as of her own world, and at the same time conveyed to his senses in an incense-like way the wide difference between them.

Potter found Lady Ella and himself drifting apart from the others. The Bishop appeared to be wrapped up in Vansittart, Lady Ella became confidential. It was not long before she had found out all about Maria.

"Bolton Gardens," she said sweetly; "I don't remember meeting your wife anywhere, Mr. Potter. I must get the Duchess to call."

This was a little vague, but none the less delightful. Potter was curious to know what duchess, but he asked no questions.

"You will be glad to get home, Lady Ella," he said.

"In a way, yes. All the same I am delighted with America. But the dear Bishop is a terrible responsibility. Nervous prostration, you know."

Potter glanced at the Bishop and expressed his sympathy. Despite his handsome face and dignified bearing the Bishop looked anything but strong.

"The sea voyage ought to set him up," he said.

"That is just what I am afraid of," Lady Ella murmured. "The racket and confusion of a long railway journey tries my poor uncle terribly. Constant rest and quietness are absolutely essential to him. It was our mistake—we thought the change and bustle would work wonders. I am so sorry we did not accept the Prince's offer, and use his steam yacht to cross the Atlantic. If I could get a special car to take us from here to New York I should feel easier; really I feel quite capable of pawning my jewels to do so. But that is impossible."

"You would feel more satisfied yourself?"

"Well, no. My nerves need no bracing, and I am looking forward to my trip on the cars. But the Bishop does not care for company, and the expense of a special car—if I could only borrow one of those belonging to those travelling American millionaires. The rest of the voyage could be nothing. But I am talking nonsense."

Potter smiled. He saw a way to clinch the matter of the apochryphal duchess and the friendly call at Bolton Gardens. Mi1lionaires have so many psychological moments from whence to pluck solid opportunities.

"You've come to the right shop," he began. "I mean that I can procure for you the very thing you require. You have perhaps heard of the Pullman built for Duke Alexis when he was doing America."

Lady Ella had. It had been specially designed for a Tartar prince desirous of new channels for the dissipation of his fortune before Monaco came in still more handy for the purpose.

"She was a dream, they tell me," said Lady Ella. "After the prince shot himself she was purchased by some billionaire. Do you know her?"

"Rather," Potter chuckled. "I bought her. Always travelling from place to place I find it a great advantage to run my own Pullman car. The last three journeys here I have made in the saloon. Anyway, she's here now doing nothing for the next few months, and if you like to take the car to New York and give the Bishop the quiet he requires, why take her and welcome, say I."

Lady Ella was touched, deeply touched by this friendly offer. She did not say that Augustus had suggested the idea. At first she could not consent to hear anything of the kind. Then she began to struggle between proper pride and her duty towards the Bishop. Should she allow sentiment to stand in the way of a man who by common consent must be the next Primate?

"Uncle shall decide," she said, "but in any case, Mr. Potter, we shall never be able to repay you this great service. Uncle, what do you think Mr. Potter says?"

The Bishop protested. He could not dream of such a thing, he said. His white slim hands were upraised against the temptress. No, he would suffer in silence, he would fight against his nervousness and conquer. Nothing could induce him to listen to such a suggestion, and then, five minutes later, like Byron's fair frail one in that most delightful of all epics:

Swearing he would ne'er consent—consented.

Potter was quite touched to see the change in the Bishop. That good man had evidently fought hard against the dread anticipation of the uncongenial journey. His kindly face became all smiles, he checked himself humming an operatic fragment. Potter glowed with the consciousness of a kindly action well done. Besides, the Primate might one day come and dine in Bolton Gardens.

"Positively, I am ashamed of myself," said the Bishop. "But I am not going to be selfish. Is there anything we can do in return? I feel that nothing could repay you for this—er—stupendous kindness. Mr. Potter, I verily believe that you have saved my reason."

Potter expressed his delight. He began to dream of himself as Lcrd Potter and of Maria as leading a salon in Bolton Gardens.

"You can't do much," he chuckled, only you might keep your eye on the expressmen on the journey. I'm going to send the 'Rosy Cross' to my bankers by your train."

Lady Ella was deeply interested. Earlier in the evening she had examined and admired that wonderful stone. She declared herself to be thrilled. "You shan't lose it if I can help it," she said.

"Good-night, Mr. Potter!"

During the next day and a-half Vansittart found it necessary to leave his relatives to their own devices in Chicago. Had they seen and watched his movements they would have been both interested and puzzled. By the next evening he was some four hundred miles by mail express along the line. There he alighted with some cases, which he proceeded to place in a buggy awaiting him. Then he drove off through the lonely country alone. Presently he struck the railway-track again at a point where some scrub growing from a deep still part hung close to the edge of the rails. The work took some two hours, but at length it was finished. When Vansittart had completed his task, some sixty feet of the scrub was covered by a strong spongy net, such as acrobats used when fired from cannons, and such-like engaging occupations. Vansittart regarded the thing with satisfaction. The perspiration poured down his face.

But he had not finished yet. Some ten miles nearer to Chicago, in an equally desolate spot, stood a cluster of tall trees, one of which Vansittart proceeded to climb with some large brass instrument in his hand. This was nothing more or less than a powerful oil lamp, which was fixed presently and lighted.

"There!" Vansittart muttered, in a self-satisfied tone, "I calculate that will burn for fifty-six hours; and nobody is likely to come along and disturb it. If they do, so much the worse for Potter. If all goes well and he does meet with an accident here, he won't come to any harm. And what a pleasant time the Bishop and Lady Ella will have afterwards."

Vansittart returned to his horses and drove back to the depot where he had alighted. There was some time to wait for a western train, but it came at length; and long before Chicago was astir, the adventurer was back again. At breakfast-time the Honourable Augustus Vansittart lounged into the private apartment of his Grace of Croydon in his most used-up condition.

"You look as if you had been working hard," Lady Ella laughed.

"Awfully," came the drawling response.

"'Pon my word, I've quite an appetite."

CHAPTER II

Within half-an-hour of the departure of the New York express a breathless individual burst, without ceremony, into Mr. Potter's office.

"My name is Barnes, and I am a detective from New York," he said. "I should have got here before only the rascals got wind of me, and I've been a prisoner for two days. They think I'm safe for a few days."

"What the deuce are you talking about?" Potter demanded.

"I'm talking about the 'Rosy Cross,'" Barnes responded drily, "and I'm talking about the dear Bishop, and Lady Ella, and the Honourable Augustus to boot. There's a very pretty plot afoot to swindle you out of your big diamond."

And Barnes proceeded to reel off a graphic story of personal abduction. He also proceeded to describe the plan for getting the big diamond from the safe.

"We must telegraph," Potter explained. "They've got my private Pullman, and—"

"The wire won't do," Barnes interrupted. "They may be safely off the train in two hours-perhaps the first stop at Fort Anson. Look here, I've got the thing all cut and dried, and if you want to keep your marble, you must do as you're told. The thieves won't recognise me in this disguise, and we shall lay hands upon them yet. You run off to the Central Depot and order a special train to be ready in half-an-hour."

"In the name of common sense, what for?"

"For you and I to pursue the fugitives. I calculate if we are off in an hour we shall catch the express at Winchester. It will be dark then, and we can step aboard the train without being noticed, only we are strangers, mind. Then you'll have to go to the office and get an authority from the Company for their man to give you the package from the safe."

"Man, you are talking like an idiot."

"Nonsense," Barnes said confidently, "a man with your money can do anything. If you mean to allow your jewel to go without an effort, why—"

But Potter was not made of that class of stuff. Within fifty-seven minutes by the watch a special engine and car pulled out of Chicago, and, what was more, Potter had the Express Company's permit in his pocket. His mind did not dwell upon Bolton Gardens now: he groaned to himself as he thought of the cost of this little adventure. And Lady Ella—

Barnes rudely interrupted these gloomy meditations.

"I had better tell you what my plans are," he said. "How I got on the track of those folks matters little. I did get on it, anyway, and I discovered what their game was. Like most of us, I wanted to get all the kudos of a single-handed capture, and that's why I didn't come to you in the first place. I'd got everything ready—there's an empty berth and a pile of personal luggage waiting for me on the express now—when they lured me away as neatly as possible, and, I suppose, deemed me to be safe for a spell. Now, my idea is this. Directly you board the train, get your property, then go along to your private saloon and drop in on those people in the most natural way. Don't make any disguise about the special—say you are bound to catch up the express so as to be in New York on a certain day. Don't bother about me at all; I shall be all right. But whatever you do, get your property. As you do so, walk away whistling 'Yankee Doodle.' That will be my signal. The rest of the programme I'll tell you later on."

Potter listened carefully to these instructions. For the next hour or two he paced the saloon restlessly, a prey to the keenest anxiety. If they were to miss the train the consequences might be serious. And there was no stop after Winchester for eight hundred miles. Barnes, on the other hand, was perfectly confident.

"I figured it all out carefully before we started," he said. "We shall have eight minutes to spare. We'll do those rascals yet."

This prophesy was fulfilled to the letter. It was quite dark by the time the special steamed into Winchester depot, and the welcome tail-lights of the express made a pleasing picture in Potter's eyes.

"Now, don't forget," Barnes whispered, "get your gem first. I can do nothing until I know that you have it safely or otherwise. I'm going to my berth. When the time comes to strike, expect me. But not before."

Barnes went straight away for his berth with the carriage of a man who knows exactly what he is doing. When he emerged into the light again, strange to say, all trace of Barnes had disappeared, and the Hon. Augustus Vansittart stood in his stead. Then he hurried along to the Pullman. As he strolled gently in Lady Ella cried out:

"Upon my word, you are too provoking," she said. "Here we have been worrying about you, and you are on the train all the time."

"I did it to punish you," said Vansittart, "you were so rude last night."

"And whose fault was that, pray?"

"Yours, of course," responded the imperturbable Augustus. "Still, I forgive you, my child. As a matter of fact, I did only catch the train by the skin of my teeth. I hope you are enjoying this unwonted splendour."

"For my part I regard it as a blessing," the Bishop said unctiously. "In the present condition of my nervous system, the absence of stir and chatter"

"The Duchess of Mayfair is aboard," Lady Ella interrupted.

Vansittart lifted his eyebrows, although he knew the fact perfectly well. The Bishop groaned, for already the Duchess had proved the one fly in the clarity of his amber, her grace being a philanthropist who regarded a prelate as her natural prey.

Someone at this moment came down the corridor whistling "Yankee Doodle."

Vansittart's eyes flashed for an instant, then they resumed their sleepy expression. Then the door was pulled aside, and a pallid face with an uneasy grin on it looked in.

"Mr. Potter," Lady Ella cried, "are you a magician or—"

"'Uman, merely 'uman," Potter murmured. "Don't wonder you are surprised to see me. Fact is, directly you had gone I got a telegram that made it necessary to get to New York without delay. I chartered a special to catch you, and here I am."

Lady Ella expressed her pleasure. If she and the Bishop were acting they were doing it marvellously well. Not the slightest sign of uneasiness was to be detected. Potter began to feel a little more at his ease. If their bearing impressed him, it seemed pretty certain that their suspicions had not been aroused. They sat chatting there for the next two hours. Then Vansittart rose under pretence of a desire to smoke. Some minutes later he looked in again.

"Sorry to disturb your little symposium," he said, "but the Duchess urgently desires to see her friend the Bishop. Shall she come here, or—"

He of Croydon rose with a smothered groan.

"No, no," he said; "of the two evils I would far rather go to her Grace. Once she invades my little sanctum my peace will be broken for the rest of the voyage. A good woman, a most devout woman, Mr. Potter; but her voice—Ella, will you accompany me? I shall get away all the sooner if you do."

Ella rose to her feet at once.

"Certainly," she said, cheerfully. "I will do anything you please. We shall be back as soon as we possibly can, Mr. Potter."

The door closed behind them. Potter measured Vansittart with his eye. The "Rosy Cross" in his pocket rendered him slightly nervous. Still, in a hand-to-hand struggle with a delicate youth like the one opposite—and Barnes was near. Vansittart drew back one of the sliding panels and stepped on to the gangway.

"It's too hot to be in there a night like this," he said.

He made no suggestion that Potter should join him, which was the reason, perhaps, why the other did so without hesitation. The express car gliding along with lightning speed, the low handrail would have been no protection in case of a struggle.

"What's that down the track yonder?" Potter asked presently. "That light."

"Don't know," Vansittart said carelessly; "it must be five or six miles away yet. Looks to me like a lantern burning on a hill."

"A signal of some kind, perhaps. All the same, I—"

Potter said no more. With a cat-like spring, Vansittart was upon him. There was not the slightest chance for the startled millionaire to cry out, for he was pinned down to the gangway with the grip of a vice, and a handkerchief drenched in some pungent smelling compound was rammed into his throat.

The next few seconds passed like a dream of minutes. Potter was vaguely conscious of nimble hands going over his pockets, of a low, pleased chuckle, and when he came to himself the gag was still in his mouth. As he scrambled to his feet, he was raised like a child and tossed over the handrail. Almost to a yard he alighted on the spot where Vansittart had intended. The scrub and moss and water broke the force of the fall. And when the discomfited millionaire rose, bruised and giddy, but otherwise unscathed, he could see the tail lamps of the express getting fainter and fainter in the night haze.

Panting and breathless from the struggle, Felix Gryde leaned against the rail. He had closed the panel behind him; he stood in a strip of black darkness. On either side of him the train emitted a stream of dazzling light.

Gryde smiled to himself, for the "Rosy Cross " was in his pocket, and his faithful beacon light flashed ahead. Not one of his carefully-laid plans had gone astray.

He heard the saloon door open, and Lady Ella's voice calling him.

"Coming," he replied. "Mr. Potter and I are discussing a little business. Don't open the slide—its fearfully dusty here."

Then Gryde stood up on the rail, and balanced himself as well as possible. As the train shot past the beacon lamp he began to count slowly up to ten.

"Neck or nothing," he muttered; "here goes!"

He launched himself with a spring into the blackness of the night. The next seconds was an eternity. Then he touched something; there was a rebound, an elastic thrill, as Gryde rolled over and over in the net. He had escaped with not so much as a single scratch.

The rest of the adventure was child's play. Gryde was not the man to leave anything undone. He knew exactly where he was and what to do next. By the time that daylight came the lantern, the net, plus the elegant Bond Street attire of the Hon. Augustus, were buried deep in a pool, and ere sunrise a typical cowboy was making his way across the plain in the direction of the thriving "city" of Birmingham.

A few days later in the Central Hotel, New York, an angry and sore—with more senses than one—millionaire was having an anything but pleasant interview with the Chief of Police, the Bishop of Croydon and Lady Ella.

"I can assure you, Mr. Potter," said the official suavely, "your friends here are as innocent as yourself. And that they are really what they represent themselves to be, I am in a position to positively prove."

"We have been grossly deceived," quoth the Bishop. "That rascal, it turns out, was no relation to us at all. My real nephew is on his way here, and until he got my cable was not aware of his good fortune. That swindler must have met my nephew, and gleaned enough family history to be able to blind us to his real character."

"And he looked like a gentleman," Potter groaned.

"Many thieves are well educated," said the Chief. "Indeed, a robbery of this kind could only have been planned and carried out by a man of marked intelligence. Probably he gleaned what you were going to do with your diamond, and the coming of the Bishop and Lady Ella to Chicago—which he could glean from the papers—gave him the inspiration. A man like that is always ready to turn opportunities to account."

Potter groaned again. Lady Ella looked sweetly sympathetic.

"He must have been clever in disuise," she said.

"You're right there," Potter moaned.

"Fancy his acting two men to me like that, and I never tumbled. And you'll never catch him either."

The Chief smiled mysteriously. It was his duty to do so, but privately he was quite of Potter's opinion. Then followed an awkward silence. Lady Ella came to the rescue in her charming way as usual.

"Well," she said, "in any case we shall never forget your kindness, Mr. Potter. And when we get home I shall most assuredly make it a point to call at Bolton Gardens. Doubtless you will forgive us in time."

Potter grasped the proffered hand.

"I'm quite sure of one thing," he said; "if I don't, my wife will."

THE DEATH OF THE PRESIDENT

CHAPTER I

"Monsieur, the proofs, the proofs are before you to witness if I lie. Ah, would that I could make use of them myself!"

"Which means that you dare not do so?" Felix Gryde asked.

The volatile little Frenchman opposite grinned uneasily. Jules Falbe was by no means a bad-looking man; he had a good address, a cultivated accent, and there, to a trained eye like Gryde's, the suggestion of forçat* was unmistakable.

[*forçat - French, convict.]

For the present Gryde occupied a handsome set of chambers in one of the most fashionable quarters of Lutetia, which, as everybody knows, is the capital of the Gallic Federated States Republic. Business of a delicate nature had brought him there; something new and audacious was to be carried out, and Gryde was now engaged in placing the keystone on the tip of the edifice. A chance word, an obscure newspaper paragraph, had given him the germ of an idea for a magnificent fraud.

With his own marvellous intellect, his superhuman skill and patience, he had unravelled the threads. Months of time and thousands in money had been expended. Every card was in Gryde's hands at length.

In the Bois beneath the stream of gaiety and fashion flowed on. Not for a quarter of a century had Lutetia presented so brilliant a spectacle. For it was the year of the colossal Exhibition, the finest the world had ever seen, which was to be opened in a week or two by the President of the Republic. At a moderate estimate, over a million wealthy strangers were in Lutetia.

Gryde crossed from the window with a smile. From head to foot he was attired in faultless black; a riband of some order was in his button-hole. His sallow face and thick, dark moustache were in keeping with the rest. He might have been a soldier of fortune or of finance, a military attaché—anything of that kind. A good many people wondered who the Chevalier Lorraine was, and what he was doing here in Lutetia.

"Why don't you try President Granville yourself?" he asked.

"Because I dare not," Falbe snarled; "I have a past, Chevalier, which is not—"

"Not altogether unconnected with Toulon.* Go on."

[* i.e. Bagne de Toulon - A notorious prison in Toulon, France.]

"And who has told the Chevalier that?"

"Never mind, you are a returned convict. It is many years ago, and since then you have never been in trouble. Who is any the wiser?"

Falbe dashed his fist passionately on the table.

"The police are," he hissed. "You forget the dossier. Ah! that accursed system; with its photographs and its measurements,and its infernal biography, there is no escape. And Granville is no better than myself."

"Most of us are guilty of indiscretions at some time or another," Gryde said soothingly. "The President, it seems from your proofs, is a kind of Gallic Prince Hal up-to-date. You say he ought to have suffered with you!"

"Ma foi, yes. That is five-and-twenty years ago. I was the catspaw and he escaped. Then he got himself conveniently drowned under his proper name, and reappeared three years later under a new description. When I came to Lutetia a year ago and saw him, I was astounded. I recognised him at once. Then I contrived to let him know that I was aware, and he was not fearful. He could crush me. Guess why?"

"Because you did not serve out your sentence at Toulon, but escaped."

"You have guessed it. You are a marvellous man. I am liable, therefore, to serve the rest of my sentence if I am discovered. And I had not then the proofs which I have placed in your hands. And why you come to me and proclaim the fact that you have probed my history, I know not."

Gryde's face expressed the most engaging frankness.

"I will tell you," he said. "Accident gave me the clue. The rest is merely a game of financial chess. You have the board and the position, but you do not possess the requisite strength to play a cunning game— I do. You are a poor man in needy circumstances, you have an idea which might be put to practical results in America if you only had the money. Therefore I am going to give you fifty thousand francs for your papers, and you leave for America without delay."

Falbe shrugged his shoulders.

"I am entirely in your hands," he said.

"Of course you are," Gryde replied coolly. "I have taken uncommonly good care of that. And I offer you your own price. Here is your passage money, and you are to depart at once. You will cross over to England and proceed to Liverpool, taking passage from there by the Lucania to New York next Thursday. Before sailing you will send me a telegram. Once arrived in New York, you can go to the National Bank and present this letter of credit, and procure cash in exchange."

Jules Falbe departed, well satisfied with his transaction. For the next day or two Gryde had nothing to do but to sit down and await developments. Faithfully as promised, Falbe sent the telegram. With a sigh of satisfaction, Gryde put on his hat and went out.

Gay and bustling with excitement as Lutetia was, evidently there was something more than usual in the air. During the last day or two the city had stirred to a new sensation. Something fresh and startling was coming; they knew not what.

A few hours before, and there had been no sign of this mysterious advent. Now every blank wall and hoarding teemed with the first breath of the mystery. Thousands of huge posters stared Lutetia in the face; posters so huge and so daringly original that they were the passing sensation of the hour. These mammoth bills were circular in shape, a dead black on a white border. In the centre of the murky desert was a white, shapely hand pointing to the single word Eros. There was absolutely nothing more.

Try as they could, curious Lutetians could learn nothing further. Was it a new pill, a patent soap, something fresh in the way of a sauce? Not a soul had seen the bills posted, none knew from whence they had come.

Gryde smiled to himself as he passed poster after poster, each surrounded by a gaping crowd. He was on his way to the Place de l'Europe, which, as most people are aware, is close to the Bourse, and a quarter where the brokers and underwriters most do congregate. Here Gryde presently entered an office, and was shown in to the head of the firm.

"I am Chevalier Lorraine," Gryde said, simply.

Monsieur Morence greeted his visitor cordially.

"O yes," he said, "I got your letter. As an underwriter, I am prepared to take up anything. You wish to insure something, I understand."

"I do," Gryde responded. "I am desirous of insuring the life of President Granville."

"Surely a most singular request."

"Not at all, M'sieur Morence. The head of the State has been frequently insured in England. Take the Diamond Jubilee, for instance. I have a great scheme on at present, what, if anything happened to the President, could ruin me. If you do not care to undertake the business, I can get it done in England."

"O, I will undertake it, of course. After all, it is legitimate trade. The premium in such cases is six per cent. In what amount would you—"

"Three million francs."

"The Chevalier must assuredly be joking!"

"The Chevalier is doing nothing of the kind," Gryde responded drily. "I understand in big risks like this you gentlemen insure one another."

"You are going to run an exhibition of your own," Morence suggested, smilingly.

"You have guessed it exactly," said Gryde. "Like most people, you have seen and shared in the excitement created by those Eros posters. Let me tell you that I am responsible for them, and that Eros will be the most extraordinary and unique entertainment ever seen. I should not wonder if it dwarfed the Exhibition entirely. Millions of people will witness that amazing spectacle. To prepare it has cost me a fortune. To-day I have taken the Imperial Theatre for three months. A fortune is in my grasp, but if anything happens to the President I am a ruined man. Lutetia would be a city of mourning for months, you understand."

Morence nodded thoughtfully. Gryde's position was perfectly logical.

"I will undertake the business," he said, "and if you will call later in the day the contract will be ready. It is, of course, a cash transaction."

"Naturally," Gryde said curtly, "and if misfortune comes my money must be paid on the nail. By the time I have given you a cheque for the premium I shall have barely enough to last till Eros bursts upon a startled world."

The man of money hastened to reassure Gryde on this point. Later in the day the big cheque was paid over and the policy taken up.

It was nearly midnight; the President had had a long trying day but he had not yet retired, he being the only person up in the house. A cigarette half-smoked had burnt out between his fingers; he pulled the long grey moustache as he restlessly paced the room. The usually placid features were given over to anxiety and care.

"Why doesn't the fellow come?" he muttered.

A few minutes later and an electric bell thrilled softly. Granville crossed the wide marble hall and flung open the door. The light streamed upon the scathe features and black muzzle of Chevalier Lorraine.

"I am late, your Excellency," said the latter.

"Devilish late," muttered the President. "Come in! come in!"

Gryde followed his distinguished host into the magnificent dining-room, taking care to close the door behind him. Without waiting for an invitation he flung himself down in a chair and faced the anxious statesman.

"You know why I am here?" he asked.

"It would be absurd to deny it," Granville said, huskily. "Reading between the lines of your letter it is easy to see that you are possessed of the one shameful secret of my life. With such proofs as you possess, a single card, and my social and political career is ended. There is one other man, but— pshaw!— he dare not speak. Your proofs, sir."

Gryde laid a packet of papers on the table.

"These are copies," he said. "For obvious reasons I have left the originals in a place of safety. Will you see that they are all as represented?"

For half an hour the President read on in silence. His lips quivered, a greyness like the hue of death lay upon his features.

"I yield," he said; "you have me in the hollow of your hand. Your price?"

"You quite mistake me," Gryde said, gravely. "I don't want any money at all. Does your Excellency mind my speaking plainly?"

"Not at all. You may be as explicit as you please."

"Thank you. In the first place I know a great deal more about you than you imagine. Beyond the secret of those papers I have proved others. Beyond your official salary your means are limited; and yet, never since the Empire, has the presidential state been kept up with such regal magnificence. Trembling from day to day upon the verge of ruin, you have had resource to speculation. In your position, with the exclusive information at your command, you could hardly lose. You are on a great venture now, which, when it is ripe a few weeks hence, will mean millions of money to you. Do not protest, because my proofs are absolute and conclusive."

"You are the devil," the President the groaned.

"A poor devil," Gryde said, with sardonic pleasantry. "But let me hasten to assure you that I shall do you no harm whatever. My silence will have to be purchased, but not with money. I have great issues at stake,and it is for you to say whether or not they shall be carried out successfully. You can help me."

"At the loss of all I hold dear, I suppose?"

"At the loss of nothing whatever. There is absolutely no risk of any description. Into the bargain you will get eight days' holiday. That you are a man of wonderful courage and resolution the past has proved. Are you agreed?"

"Yes, yes. Only tell me all and end this awful suspense."

Gryde crossed over, and for ten minutes whispered rapidly in the President's ear. Amazement and incredulity struggled for mastery on the latter's face, and yet at the same time he seemed to be more than half convinced.

"Did anyone ever hear of anything so mad-brained outside the realm of farce," he cried, "and yet it seems to me that safety lies that way."

"The thing is absolutely safe," said Gryde. "You will guess that I shall profit by the comedy; indeed, I have worked it all out to a nicety. Afterwards I pledge my word to trouble you no more. As to the drug, I had the same direct from one of those wonderful old Indian fakirs. I did not take his word for it, but tried it on myself with perfect results."

"And for eight days—"

"The stuff did all that was claimed for it. Within four-and-twenty hours you will have ample time to carry out the line of action I have foreshadowed, you can leave behind you all the directions you desire, and when the psychological moment arrives, somebody will be there to give the alarm and call for assistance."

"Somebody you can rely upon, I sincerely trust?"

"Assuredly," Gryde responded drily, "seeing that I can trust myself."

The President rose to his feet. The old light of the battle sparkled in his eyes. He reached out for Gryde's hand and grasped it warmly.

"It shall be done," he said, "and the sooner the better. I will see that those papers are drawn up to-morrow, and at the same hour you shall come here with the—"

Gryde nodded. He perfectly understood. Then he rose to go. As he passed along the now deserted moonlit streets in the direction of his chambers he passed several of the now famous Eros posters. There was a peculiar smile on his face.

"Artistic," he muttered, "and represent a hundred thousand per cent each. No picture-dealer ever made such a profit before."

Late the next night, when the door had once more closed upon Felix Gryde, the President of the Gallic Federated States retired slowly to his room. Once undressed, he took from a pocket a tiny phial, the cork of which he drew. Then he proceeded to make a hollow in the huge fire glowing in the grate. His knees knocked together, but his face was stern and resolute. Throwing back his head he poured the contents of the phial into his mouth, dropped the bottle into the heart of the ruddy core and beat the coals down. With a spring he leapt into bed, at the same time swallowing down the tasteless fluid. Immediately a cold shiver ran through every limb.

"Great God!" Granville cried, "I'm—I'm dying. That rascal has—"

His teeth snapped together like a pistol shot. A flash of lightning seemed to strike him between the eyes, and the rest was silence.

CHAPTER II

Lutetia woke the next morning to the glad consciousness of a perfect day. A great review was to be held in one of the parks; the President would be present, and Lutetia had made up her mind to make the day one of pleasure. By eleven o'clock the cafés and restaurants along the principal boulevards were crowded. Care and trouble had been beaten off for the present; gaiety sparkled from thousands of bright eyes. Then, apparently as if by magic, everything changed.

An uneasy rumour ran through the crowd. Something fateful had happened. In some vague way the name of the President had found vent from trembling lips. An army of newsboys came charging along, rending the air with raucous cries.

"Death of the President! Sudden death of the President! Full details."

A charge was made for the papers. In the struggle in front of the Café Globe Gryde got one. With less curiosity than the rest he perused it.

SUDDEN DEMISE OF PRESIDENT GRANVILLE
THE PRESIDENT IS FOUND DEAD IN HIS BED THIS MORNING
HEART DISEASE THE CAUSE

It is with feelings of the deepest regret and the most profound sorrow that we have to announce the appallingly sudden death of his Excellency the President. All we can glean up to the present is that when Maurice, his Excellency's valet, went to call his illustrious master this morning at seven, he was overwhelmed to find that the head of the Republic had passed away peacefully in his sleep.

Later details to hand point to the fact that signs of the end were not wanting. We hear that his Excellency has had one or two alarming fainting fits lately, followed by a coma very like death itself. Further particulars will be given in the next edition.

In the twinkling of an eye Lutetia had been plunged into mourning. By nightfall the better informed papers had obtained all information. They even made known extracts from the late ruler's will which had been found, signed only the previous day, in his bed-chamber.

The President, it appeared, had a morbid horror of being buried alive. His instructions gave orders for a pierced coffin closed but not screwed down, and also that he should be buried in the vault purchased by him some time before. It was a little singular, said the papers, that death should so speedily have followed upon the penning of the gruesome orders.

Gryde followed every line of these details carefully. On every side signs of grief and woe were to be seen. As a spectacle the funeral of President Granville was likely to become a record amongst pageants of the kind.

As might naturally have been expected, the tragic event practically ended, for the time being at least, the Exhibition festivities. From a commercial point of view it meant ruin to many of the leading shopkeepers. Many establishments closed altogether, the theatres were deserted, and the Exhibition grounds presented the most dreary spectacle. As for the Eros excitement, it seemed to have passed from the public mind like a dream.

And yet Gryde did not appear to be in the least cast down. It suited him exactly that the thing should be forgotten. As a spectator he attended the funeral of the late President—perhaps the only one in the vast crowd who viewed the pomp and ceremony with feelings of equanimity.

On the morrow shops were opened again, and business of a kind resumed. But there were plenty of signs to denote the fact that the great Exhibition year was doomed to be a ghastly failure. Gryde lost no time in waiting upon Morence. He found the latter gloomily drawing skeletons on his blotting-pad. Nothing was doing; the exchanges were deserted. The disaster amounted to a financial Sedan.

"I have been expecting you," Morence said, with a sigh.

"Naturally," Gryde responded drily. "I presume that on Saturday morning my little matter will be settled."

"O, yes; the terms of the policy will be faithfully carried out. I shall have to see one or two of my partners. As you are aware, nobody would take such a risk alone. You have hit a dozen or so of us heavily."

"The fortune of war," Gryde responded.

"O, I am not complaining. I suppose Lutetia is not likely to see anything of your wonderful show when you have this money."

Gryde puffed at his cigarette thoughtfully.

"Well, I am not so sure of that," he responded. "You people are exceedingly volatile, and you may shake this off in a few days. Anyway, I can afford to wait here a few weeks and see now. My entertainment is not going to be produced anywhere in anything but a gala season."

"I suppose you won't mind giving self and partners an order?"

Gryde duly responded to the sardonic humour, and departed. Punctual to the moment, he turned up on the Saturday and took his heavy cheque with the air of a man who habitually handles millions.

No sooner was the same received than it was paid into an account opened elsewhere in the name of Chevalier Lorraine, and thence depleted by cheques payable in various capitals of Europe. By the time the cheques were all manipulated, it would have been impossible to trace a tithe of the money. This being so, it might be assumed that Gryde had finished, and that this apparent stroke of luck would have sufficed for the present adventure.

But there were several things to be accomplished yet. Sunday dawned bright and fine, with some little sign of life in Lutetia and a semblance of subdued gaiety on the boulevards. Gryde saw nothing of this, for during the whole of the afternoon and far into the evening he was busy writing.

By this time night had fallen. The house was strangely quiet, as indeed it might have been, since Gryde had got rid of all the servants under one pretext or another. He threw his pen away with a feeling of satisfaction.

"And now," he said gaily, "now to put money into the purse of the world of journalism. Upon my word, the gentlemen of the press ought to be profoundly grateful to me. But out of all the sensations I have given them, I doubt if any one of them can come near to the drama about to be performed to-night."

Gryde proceeded to lock the door. Then he took from a safe the materials for a picturesque, if somewhat forbidding disguise. A little later there slipped out into the street a typical Lutetian ragpicker.

Thus attired, Gryde took his way rapidly in the direction of the Maratan cemetery. Once there, he proceeded to make his stand by the vault covering the remains of President Granville. The grass was trampled down around, a pile of fading flowers graced the granite. The iron grating had not yet been bricked up.

Nobody was in sight. Gryde bent down and listened intently. Then the rigid anxiety of his lips changed. A moment later and there rang out across the marbled silence a scream of horror and agony.

Footsteps came towards Gryde; out of the gloom loomed a keeper or two, and the stiff rigidity of a couple of gens d'arme. They gripped the mendicant rudely.

"Are you mad, fellow?" one of them demanded.

"No, no!" said Gryde, hoarsely, "there is someone in the vault. I came here to drop a flower, and I heard knocking. Listen!"

One braver than the rest was first to recover himself. Crowbars and picks were procured, and the vault forced open. After a little natural hesitation the lid of the coffin also was forced from its fastenings. As it fell away there was a whirl of something white and diaphanous, a sinewy, nervous hand tore bandages away like paper, and then, with a yell of horror, a ghostly figure darted up the steps.

"Frightened to death," Gryde muttered, "fearful lest I should forget him. And a few hours of that would try even me. But he'll be all right presently."

Alone Gryde left the corner of the dead. To discard his disguise that fitted him like a skin over the rest of his garments was easy. From a distant street came a roar and a yell that baffled description. In the midst of a dense throng, a figure in uniform, a General of Division and member of the Cabinet, had grappled with a lunatic who seemed to have escaped from the tomb. The meeting was purely a chance one. Then, as they panted for breath, their eyes met.

General Perry gave a scream: agony, fear, rung in the notes.

"Great heavens!" he cried, "am I mad, or dreaming? It is the President."

The words were taken up on every side. Granville fell into the arms of his colleague.

"Get me away from here and into the light," he said; "let me have light for the love of God, and save my reason. I have been buried alive. I would not go through the last few hours for Paradise itself."

Whatever was the meaning of the mystery, President Granville told nobody. Of that strange sleeping potion producing the coma of death he said nothing. For a whole week the drama rang from one side of the sphere to the other. And yet, strange to say, the deus ex machina, the ragpicker, was not to be found. Neither was Chevalier Lorraine, and to this day Lutetia knows not Eros.

Morence alone was puzzled. That astute financier had never been so bewildered in his life. It was Lorraine's bounden duty to refund that money, and no legal steps were spared to bring him to justice. But the police have not found him yet, nor are they likely to do so. That he had been made the victim of some marvellous swindle Morence felt certain. And yet to explain it...

"Three million francs," he moaned when the truth dawned upon him. "That rascal must have known something. And yet, to carry it out so successfully the President would have had to have been party to the conspiracy — which, when one comes to think of it, is ridiculous."

And, meanwhile, Felix Gryde was still in Lutetia, and on two occasions heard the puzzled financier relate his grievous transaction across the walnuts and the wine.

THE CRADLESTONE OIL MILLS

CHAPTER I

Gryde watched his companion with frank admiration. He could afford to do this openly for the simple reason that the other man was blind. All the same, Gryde never was a tight hand at a bargain where he could see his way clear to a profitable termination. Frank Chasemore must have been a handsome man before the terrible accident which had scored his face like a dried walnut and deprived him of his sight.

"I am disposed to purchase your invention," Gryde said thoughtfully.

Chasemore smiled bitterly. Gryde had picked up the clever mechanical engineer literally out of the gutter in New York. Wild and visionary as some of his schemes were, Gryde had not been slow to see the practical vein beneath.

"Let me congratulate you," Chasemore replied. "I have hawked that invention all over the States, frequently walking from town to town, and everybody laughed at me. I tell you the thing is workable—with a drill and a motor like mine I could bore a hole through the universe in a fortnight. And what is the cost? Practically nothing. But for that nitro-glycerine explosion I should have made it go. Without my eyes I am like a child. I shall have to go into the poor-house, I suppose. And yet, blind as I am, with a small competency behind me, I could startle the world yet. If the fools would only listen!"

Chasemore shook with the bitterness of his indignation. Gryde perfectly understood Was he not also a genius in his way?

"The fools are going to listen," the latter said quietly. "Do you know why I brought you and your lares to this howling wilderness?"

"I don't know," said Chasemore; "out of pure kindness, perhaps. I have read of people in books committing eccentricities of the kind."

"My dear fellow, there is no occasion for bitterness. I brought you here so that we could test your invention without attracting undue attention. If the thing succeeds in doing what you claim for it, I'll make you a present of twenty thousand dollars. That is merely for the hire of the concern, of course."

Chasemore expressed his satisfaction. If Gryde had anything in the way of a boring operation on, the patent could do the work of a regiment in less time than the same could grapple with a yard.

"So much the better for you," Gryde replied. "Now will you briefly explain."

"To outline the thing is easy. In the first place I have an entirely new motor. In the space of a pill-box I have one horse-power. The fools say you can't multiply power. When the egotist fails at a thing he always says it can't be done. Did you ever see a crowd push down a solid stone wall without anyone being hurt?"

"Get to the point," Gryde suggested quietly.

"I beg your pardon. My motor is more or less a pocket affair. With it I can drive a six-inch drill through granite at the rate of thirty feet an hour. Outside the drill runs a flexible metal coil, and between the two, by a linotype kind of smelting arrangement, I can cast and force in my pipe. What do you think of that? Thirty feet of solid tubing six inches in diameter in an hour."

Gryde's eyes glittered. It was not the first time he had heard these details. Within a day of doing so he had seen his way to turn the discovery to account. Within a week he and Chasemore had found themselves settled in a little hut in one of the loneliest and most dreary parts of Pennsylvania. There was no town in sight, nothing but a collection of wooden huts, a few long warehouses, and two tall grimy chimneys. They were within a mile of one of the greatest oil-wells in the world.

Outside the limits of the Cradlestone Syndicate Estate—itself no more than a square mile—many a bold speculator had ruined himself sinking for oil. There were shafts and pits there down which thousands of dollars had been cast. And yet whilst the Cradlestone Creek flowed like a sea, not a drop came elsewhere.

"Is it oil you are after?" Chasemore asked.

"What put that idea into your head?" Gryde demanded.

"I can't see, but I can smell," Chasemore said sententiously. "The air reeks with it. Still, your business is no business of mine. Pay in my price and I ask no questions."

"All the same you have guessed it," said Gryde. "There is oil here, but one must go down deep to find it. That is why I require your drill. I have purchased some land here with a shaft or two upon it. You will show me how to use your machine, and as for the rest you can lie here and dream to your heart's content."

Gryde, for reasons of his own, said nothing of their proximity to the Cradlestone Estate. In carrying out one of the most daring of his schemes, the blindness of Chasemore was an important and convenient factor. Fortune had favoured him again. But then Fortune always does seem to favour the man who has capital, energy, and an amazing faculty for taking pains.

"What you ask is a very easy matter," said Chasemore. "Within three days you will understand the thing as well as I do myself. And already I can see improvement..."

Chasemore's speech trailed off into a mutter. A look of dreamy speculation lay like a mist upon his face. When Chasemore retired thus within himself Gryde might as well have been alone. He lighted a cigarette and passed into the open.

So far as he could see the place was one level plain. Nothing seemed to grow there beyond the coarse bush grass. Here and there mounds of earth thrown up testified to the barren labour of the unlucky speculator. By reason of these open shafts the place was a dangerous one for the stranger after nightfall.

Gryde walked on until he reached the split rail fence bounding the Cradlestone property. From where he stood he was within four hundred yards of the main derrick. Here the ground trended down abruptly. In the centre of a hollow cup was a disused shaft. In depth it might have been two hundred feet; the winch and steel hawser for lifting purposes were still intact. Over the same stood a crazy sign bearing the legend—"Guaranteed Oil Trust." For this well astute Gryde had paid down the sum of ninety dollars cash.

Using the timber props as a means of descent, Gryde reached the bottom. The shaft was a fairly large one and perfectly dry. There was nothing there at present beyond a lantern and box of matches. By the aid of the former Gryde proceeded to examine a mass of figures. The study of these seemed to fill him with profound satisfaction.

"Four hundred yards," he muttered, "twelve hundred feet at thirty feet per hour, say three hundred feet a day. Four days would be quite sufficient. That drunken geologist who worked at this for me understood his business. Really, a child couldn't go wrong with these instructions. No rise or fall, but merely a straight boring. The three weeks I spent grappling with the mysteries of the theodolite were not spent in vain. With any luck I ought to make a clear million out of this thing."

Gryde emerged to the surface again. As he did so he became aware of the fact that he was not alone. A big man with a square, determined jaw was regarding him derisively.

"Good evening," Gryde said tentatively.

"Good evening, stranger," came the reply. "If it isn't a rude question, what's your game?"

Gryde explained. He hoped to succeed, he said, where others had failed. The other smiled.

"Do you know who I am?" he asked.

"Perfectly well," Gryde said coolly.

"You are Walter Cradlestone, the Oil King, and you are worth a hundred million dollars. You ought to be satisfied with that, but some people can never have enough. You are a lucky man, Cradlestone.".

"You're an original one, anyway," the millionaire laughed. "You'll get no oil there. Our big spring draws all the tributaries to it like a blister. I've known oil found here to spurt for a day or two and then to pour out for good. But as for quantities!"

"I don't want quantities," said Gryde: "a small supply could suffice for me, and the cruder the better. Don't suppose I've come along here to run a rival syndicate. I've got an invention, and I want my own springs to work it. We know nothing about petroleum yet."

"I guess I do," Cradlestone said drily.

"You think so, of course. All you rich men are so amazingly egotistical. I'm not thinking of oil as an illuminating power, but as a healing factor."

"Pooh. Every schoolboy has heard of vaseline."

"Granted. But if you put 'crysoline' to them they would be stumped. And crysoline is going to be one of the healers of the future. Got a bruise about you?"

Cradlestone pulled up his sleeve and displayed an ugly-looking mark on his arm.

"Pinched in a bit of machinery," he said. "Black, isn't it? And a good opening for your crysoline."

By way of reply, Gryde took a small bottle from his pocket. Inside the bottle was some jelly-like substance with a blue-grey green tinge. With the tip of his finger he applied a small portion of this to the wounded arm.

"Now pull your sleeve down," he said, "and forget all about it for a minute or two. So you think I am going to drop my money here?"

"I'm absolutely certain of it."

"Then you're as absolutely wrong, for the simple reason that I haven't any money to drop. And I don't mind making you a small bet that I shall find what I want. Now will you oblige me by pulling up your sleeve again?" Cradlestone did as desired. To his amazement he could see no trace of the dark bruise. The cut remained, but all the discoloration had vanished.

"Well!" he exclaimed, " I should like to know how that was worked."

"Crysoline," Gryde smiled. "Petroleum jelly plus—What do you think of it?"

"I think there's a mighty big fortune squeezed into that little bottle of yours. I'll give you—"

"Twopence-halfpenny for a million," Gryde laughed. "You'd like to buy the universe and sell it in shilling tins, you would. My secret is not for sale, sir."

Gryde was not to be shaken. He returned to the hut whistling.

"I've drawn the feather over his eye," he thought; "he won't suspect anything now. But unless I am greatly mistaken, Cradlestone will sing a different tune ere long. And Heaven help the man who comes to gratify his curiosity here!"

CHAPTER II

A darknes that could be felt brooded over the desolate flats around the Cradlestone estate. Walking amongst those open shafts was a matter attended by personal danger. But Gryde passed along fearlessly, leading Chasemore by the hand.

By means of a simple yet ingenious arrangement Gryde had got rid of the risk. From the hut to the dry shaft where operations were about to be commenced a length of twine had been attached. To follow this was perfectly easy.

"Why this extraordinary secrecy?" Chasemore grumbled.

"It is absolutely necessary," Gryde responded. "We are strangers in a wild place, amongst a reckless and ignorant set of men. As you remarked on a previous occasion, my business is no business of yours. But I don't mind telling you this: I am going to use your machinery to revolutionise all industries of this kind. It would mean the saving of hundreds of hands yonder. If I am found out our lives are not worth a day's purchase."

The fluent lie satisfied Chasemore. He suffered himself to be led along until the head of the shaft was reached. He trusted himself implicitly to Gryde.

"You have conveyed all machinery to the foot?" he asked.

"Everything; and a nice task it was. I had to take the stuff a bit at a time so as not to incur any notice. But it is all there now, including the petroleum necessary to start the motor. I shall have to carry you down on my back."

Chasemore naturally demurred to this proposal, but there was no other way; and, as Gryde pointed out, otherwise the contract on the former's part would not be completed.

"There is really no reason why I should put you to this trouble a second time," said Gryde, in conclusion. "If your machinery is as simple as you say it is, I ought to get the hang of the whole thing in one long lesson. Come on."

The descent was indeed a perilous undertaking. In the first place the shaft was dark as Erebus, and to find his way from one cross-beam to another with a dead weight on his shoulders tested Gryde's nerves and strength to the uttermost. Trembling violently and aching in every muscle, Gryde at length reached the bottom.

"Thank goodness that is over," he panted.

Chasemore said nothing. He could see the faint glimmer of the lantern before his sightless eyes. Then Gryde climbed half-way to the lift again and drew a curtain across the shaft . No prying eye was intended to see what was going on there.

"Now we can make a start," Gryde said, cheerfully. "I've unpacked all the boxes. Perhaps you will tell me where to begin."

Considering his infirmity, Chasemore proceeded to do so with marvellous lucidity and point. A touch of his fingers was sufficient to show him what was required. Gryde watched the curious, compact little machine being built up as a child elucidates a puzzle. Within an hour the thing was completed. Chasemore's fears were now merged with his enthusiasm.

"Now then," he exclaimed, "light the petroleum lamp. In a few minutes the pressure will be full upon the drill. If you require the tunnel made to be lined—"

"I don't require anything of the kind," Gryde interposed. "The rock is too solid to render anything of the kind necessary."

"In that case we can dispose with the more complicated part of the machinery. You see the drill can be forced forward or drawn back by this thread, which is practically endless. As to the rest, the motor is compressed air, but air compressed in a form and strength never before known. Place the drill in any spot you want it: I am ready to begin." Gryde forced the head of the drill against the side of the shaft in the direction of the Cradlestone derrick. Chasemore proceeded to pull a lever.

"You have the twelve-inch bore on," he said.

"I think it will be necessary," Gryde replied. "You keep to your part of the contract."

Chasemore shrugged his shoulders. It was all the same to him. As the machinery began to work, a flexible, hollow steel tube attached to the base of the drill began to expand as it ran off a reel. With marvellous force the drill revolved, screaming and smoking as it cut its way into the solid rock as if it had been decayed cheese. With a feeling of something like fascination, Gryde watched the process. At the end of an hour he looked at the index on the reel. Chasemore had not in any way exaggerated. Over thirty feet had been bored away.

"Are you satisfied?" Chasemore cried.

His face was aglow with enthusiasm. Gryde expressed his entire approbation. At this rate within a few days his project would be accomplished.

"You have fully earned your money," he said.

"That is good hearing," Chasemore replied. "And now, as I have no particular desire to risk my neck down this hole again, I had better show you how to work the thing. An apt pupil like yourself will pick it up in no time."

By the time daylight began, to creep out of the mist, Gryde was perfect. He turned down the petroleum lamp, and the machinery lapsed sullenly into silence.

"We must get back," he said; "it is nearly morning. A little carelessness on our part and all the labour will be lost."

An hour later and both lay fast asleep on the floor of the hut. Night was turned into day for the next week. And whilst Gryde worked in secret like a mole underground, Chasemore dreamed of the fame and fortune awaiting him when once the twenty thousand dollars were his.

Gryde was puzzled and perplexed. Angry lines criss-crossed on his forehead. After all the months of care and trouble expended, it looked as if all his plans had failed at the crucial moment. And yet he could discover nothing wrong in his data or his drawings. To make the matter no longer a mystery, Gryde had worked out to a mathematical certainty his ability, with the aid of the drill, to strike the great Cradlestone Oil Spring at a point where it entered the shaft. The calculations showed the length and direction of the boring to an inch. And once this was done, more than half the oil—the whole of it, perhaps—would flow into the new channel.

The moment had arrived. Like some uneasy, grimy demon, Gryde stood by the side of the machine, listening intently. Three feet more and he must be into the distant shaft. He checked the speed of the engine.

Another ten minutes, and he would hear the result. Once the open was found, the drill would fall spent and useless on the other side. This would be the signal that the task had at length been successfully accomplished. The seconds dragged on: Gryde could hear the beating of his own heart

"Pshaw!" he muttered; "I've been slaving away at this thing till my nerves are out of order. I never realised I had any before. And yet the moment is exciting enough in all conscience. If the drill does not— Hullo!"

The drill suddenly plunged forward, tearing the tube almost to pieces. The distant shaft had been pierced. With a breathless eagerness Gryde wound the coil reversely. Then he waited for the in-rush of oil.

It came, but only with one spurt, and then stopped. Gryde was equally puzzled and astonished. He knew that he was deep down in the spring. Why, then, did not the oil flow? A little cogitation solved the problem.

A syphon was required to start it. The up-rush of air drove the petroleum back to its own old vent. If the derrick on the far side could only be stopped for five minutes! After that they could run their pumps as long as they liked.

"Only partially successful," Gryde muttered. "If I could only close that derrick, it then would only be an explosion of—ah!"

A brilliant idea flashed into Gryde's nimble brain. Without further ado he climbed out of the shaft and took his way to the cottage. Chasemore was just beginning to stir uneasily after his night's sleep.

"Well," he asked, "have you been successful?"

"I have and I haven't," Gryde replied.

"I've reached the spot, right enough, but unfortunately I came upon a vacuum—an underground cave, probably. Therefore the drill drops into water, I expect. If you could rig me up some kind of infernal machine that I could push into the vacuum with the drill, I may manage. I want a time torpedo. Can you do it?"

"I've got the materials, right enough, in one of my boxes yonder," Chasemore said thoughtfully, "and, given one thing, I could make you a nitro-cordite package enough to blow up a town."

"And what is the one thing you lack?"

"Machinery to fire the percussion."

"What kind of machinery do you require?"

"A common American clock would do as well as anything. Or, to make a still more handy parcel, I could manage much better with a watch."

Gryde promptly took his watch from his pocket. It was a valuable gold chronometer of English make, and would have been cheap anywhere at a hundred pounds.

"Take it," he said; "the difficulty is soon overcome. "When will it be ready?"

"Not before sundown, if I am to run no unnecessary risks. Shall I make it half an hour?"

"Say an hour. I shall have to carry the thing to the shaft?"

"Yes; and you must lower it down carefully. If it should happen to fall in a certain direction I should lose my twenty thousand dollars."

Gryde nodded. He was half-dead for want of sleep. He fell heavily upon a pile of blankets in one corner of the hut, and was asleep instantly. When he came to himself again the lamp was alight on the table, and Chasemore was bending over him.

"I must have had a long sleep," Gryde said.

"Thirteen hours without a motion. I have your machine ready. Will you eat?"

Gryde hastily swallowed some food. On the table stood a square box about some six cubic inches. Outside the intense darkness had fallen once more. Gryde was eager as a schoolboy to be off and test his deadly toy.

It was fairly early yet, and a gang of men were just leaving work. Gryde could discern their ghostly forms in the distance, and the knowledge that life would be spared filled him with a certain satisfaction. He was not sorry when at length the infernal machine was safely in the boring and being gently pressed forward by the drill. Presently the latter ceased to go forward, and Gryde knew that the deed was done.

"Ah!" he said with a shudder, "it's like dancing on a volcano. I'll stay here and see the result If it fails, I must abandon my enterprise."

He waited. The seconds seemed to drag like hours. Had the machine gone wrong? Gryde wondered. He turned from the opening of the boring where he had stood listening intently, and this movement saved his life. Hardly had he done so when a mighty rushing wind came driving along the pipe carrying stones and chips of rock before it. The force of the blast whirled Gryde from his feet, and as he fell heavily to the ground a fragment of rock struck him with stunning force.

For a few seconds Gryde lay there unconscious. When he came to himself again he was floating on a seething, boiling stream of petroleum which came pouring from the pipe with a roar like that of a veritable Niagara.

Gryde had been successful. The force of the explosion had turned the current of the big spring, and the adventurer was struggling for life in the volume of his own riches. The oily mass rose with alarming rapidity, Gryde floating upwards with it. There was little or no room to swim then; he could only tread like a dog, and fight to get to the cross-beams.

When his strength was, to all practical purposes, spent, Gryde succeeded. He managed, by an effort of his iron will, to reach the surface, and for a little time he remembered no more. When he opened his eyes again it seemed as if day had returned. And yet the great sheet of flickering light before him had not the steadfast glare of sunshine. Gryde tottered to his feet and looked around.

Reaching far into the midnight sky not far away was a large pyramid of flickering flames. Its roar drowned the cries of the dancing demons around. Gryde had little trouble in guessing what had happened. He had tapped the lower depth of the petroleum while the rest had been fired by the explosion of the infernal machine. It might be weeks before that acre of blazing cloud was damped down.

"I've done it!" Gryde cried exultingly.

"I've got all the oil, and they will have none; and they will have to come to me for terms. They can buy me out if they like—indeed, I shouldn't know what to do with the stuff otherwise—but not a penny under four million dollars do I take for my property. And when one comes to think of all the trouble and worry I've had to go through, the money's worth it."

Gryde strode back to the hut in a curiously triumphant frame of mind. Chasemore was asleep. This was a pleasant surprise, because it enabled Gryde to get rid of his petroleum-soaked garments and destroy them. All Chasemore subsequently heard was that the experiment had been successful, and that they were to proceed by to-morrow's stage on the first part of their journey to the South. "And then," said Gryde, "you shall have your money."

Chasemore was too satisfied to ask any further questions.

In the morning Gryde was early astir. He did not feel entirely at ease until he had dispatched Chasemore off by the coach. There was no idea of defrauding him of his money. Nobody over at the wells had any idea that Gryde had a companion, neither was the latter anxious to have the fact blazoned on the housetops.

"Something detains me," he said. "I will pick you up at Bedford. Wait at the hotel there for me, and pay for your requirements out of this bill."

Hardly had the cloud of dust caused by the coach subsided, when there came towards the hut the visitor Gryde had expected. The latter was quite easy in his mind, Chasemore could never by any means guess the truth.

Cradlestone's face was a study in suppressed passions. The millionaire was mad with rage.

"You scoundrel," he cried, "how did you manage it? O, you know precious well what I mean. I had a great mind to shoot you in your tracks."

"I have my revolver in my hand behind me," Gryde said quietly. "I expected some such folly as this, and that is why I waited. I have only taken advantage of a little geological knowledge, which but for that explosion yonder would have been useless. It is the fortune of war. A little time ago you had the oil and I had the hole, and now the positions are reversed. If you can prove that I have done you a wrong you have your remedy."

"I can't prove it," Cradlestone said sullenly.

"But you may get a jury to believe that I dug a hole a quarter of a mile through the granite with a toothpick," Gryde smiled. "Or you might pump my shaft and find something unique in the way of machinery. I'll sell it."

"Ah, I suppose you would require half a million—"

"Four million dollars cash within a week, or it goes elsewhere. You came here to make terms: those are mine. And all the time you are smiling in that superior way you are thinking what a fool I am for my pains."

"Four million dollars is a lot of money."

"And a ruined concern like yours is worth nothing."

"Very well. You shall have your price. If you can contrive to see me, say, this day week, at our New York office, we can arrange the matter. I can only hope you are not going to take so much money out of the country."

Gryde smiled meaningly.

"No," he said, " I am going to try my luck on Wall Street. You need not laugh. Your smart brokers will not get the best of me, I promise you. I shall do them."

"As you have done me, if I only knew how," Cradlestone muttered. "Good-day."

REDBURN CASTLE

CHAPTER I

Quite a nice little sensation was caused early last season by what was known at the time as the Angela Love incident. Miss Love was a lady who had speedily distinguished herself upon the stage for her remarkable beauty, the daintiness of her pose, and the exceeding sweetness of her smile. Captain Love had been a prominent figure in his time, and when Angela found herself a penniless orphan, she took to the boards as the quickest and easiest way of making a living.

That she was absolutely no actress made no difference to her ultimate success. For the rest she was a brainless, utterly selfish little doll, with a fine talent for the pleading-pathetic branch of flirtation, and ere three months were over a dozen men were ready to cut each other's throats for her sake.

Conspicuous amongst Angela Love's admirers stood the young Duke of Redburn. Up to his twentieth year this young sprig of nobility had been nourished under the wing of a Puritanic grandmother in the seclusion of Redburn Castle, one of the finest and most picturesque residences on the Yorkshire coast. There was a fine vein of the ancient chivalry in Redburn's blood; he was raw and romantic, and once he made the acquaintance of Miss Love, he fell into her toils directly.

According to the quidnuncs, there was only one thing that prevented the lady from becoming Duchess of Redburn instanter. Redburn was poor for a duke, and the pretty actress had a fine eye for the substantial. Also, there was another keen admirer in the person of Wellington Mills, a young millionaire whose parental millions had been dug out somewhere in the coaly North.

Meanwhile it was a little difficult for Angela Love to make up her mind. By way of making matters secure, she hit upon the happy expedient of becoming engaged to both men at the same time— a profound secret, of course.

And equally, of course, the inevitable happened. A very pretty quarrel took place at the Flaneurs' Club without damaging the lady in the eyes of the two swains, the upshot of the whole business being a duel a day or two later with pistols on the sands at Trouville, in which fray Redburn lost his left arm.

The next post after this Homeric contest brought letters to each of the combatants from Angela Love. She was very much annoyed, she said, at what had taken place, and being unable to decide between the two fiery knights, had solved the Gordian knot by marrying Prince Doddlekin, who, incidentally, is one of the richest men in Europe. Princess Doddlekin is to-day a prominent figure in society and adores her Tartar husband, who, it is said, beats her upon times. Angela is the class of woman who always admires that kind of man.

Wellington Mills swore by all his gods to abjure the sex henceforward, and six months later led to the altar Lady Amelia Bulfinch, only daughter of Lord Lockland. On the other hand, Redburn took the thing far more to heart. He started without delay for the far West of America on a hunting expedition, leaving strict orders behind him that no letters or papers of any kind were to be forwarded for a year.

All this was accordingly set out at length in The Lyre and The Universe, and for seven subsequent numbers the rival editors quarrelled over petty details, and agreeing upon one fact only—that the Duke of Redburn had really gone.

Few people followed this little romance with more interest than Felix Gryde. He had read something of it in a New York paper, and it had been his privilege to see on a Western-going express his Grace of Redburn with a small arsenal in charge of his man. Gryde had met with a nasty accident and was proceeding homewards to recuperate. With a swift change of plans, he at once joined the Western train and contrived to spend a day or two in Redburn's company. The upshot of this will be seen presently. Before finally leaving New York, Gryde posted to England a couple of letters copied from a specimen of handwriting in his possession which caused him infinite pains and trouble.

Nine days later he astonished and delighted Cora Coventry by a call. Most people were out of town by this time. Cora pined, neglected, scarcely knowing where to go. And now Gryde had changed the whole aspect of affairs.

"You are looking wretchedly ill," said Cora.

"I am ill," Gryde responded. "I want a thorough change—a big comfortable country house, a little shooting, and a bracing sea air. But all my capital is out ground-baiting at present, and I have no money to spare. Still, I can see a way."

"You always can," Cora murmured admiringly.

"A way to a few months in a grand old castle where we can fare on the best at no expense whatever to ourselves. You have a very pretty talent for playing a part, Cora, and you have also spent a year or two in America. Are you ready?"

"Am I ready!" Cora cried. "I am ready for anything to vary this monotony, and I can always rely upon you where there is any real danger. What is your plan, Paul?"

As may be remembered, Gryde was Paul Manners to Cora Coventry.

"Extremely simple," Gryde exclaimed.

"I am a wealthy American, Cyrus B. Coventry. I have of late made my pile in the States, and I have come over to see my sister. You may have a rich brother in the States for anything one knows to the contrary. So, on the whole, you had better remain as you are—if danger arises it will make the escape all the easier for you, as I will explain presently. Cyrus Coventry will call upon you to-morrow, properly dressed for the part, and you will receive him with open arms."

"Good !" Cora cried. "What fun it will be! And where are we going?"

"We are going to take Redburn Castle for six months," Gryde said gravely. "To-morrow you and I will go together to call upon the agents. Everything is arranged, and you will find the whole thing as easy as possible. What time shall you be ready?"

Cora announced that eleven o'clock would suit her perfectly, and Gryde departed. When he made his appearance the following morning Cora scarcely recognised him. He was American of the best type to the life; even his expression of face had changed.

"Guess you are ready," he said with a slight drawl. "And you're coming along with me to fix up things with the Duke's agent. I've got a car outside."

Cora allowed herself to go with the tide, and a little later she and Gryde found themselves in Cheapside. In Ironmonger Lane were situated the offices of Messrs. Sutton and Co., in whose hands, more or less, all the property in England is manipulated. In a careless, off-hand kind of way Gryde produced a neat card bearing the legend, "Cyrus B. Coventry, Langham Hotel." After a slight delay, he and Cora found themselves ushered up the stairs into the office of one of the partners.

"I expect you know my business?" said Gryde.

Mr. Martin Sutton took up a letter from his table.

"O, yes," he said. "I have been expecting you, Mr. Coventry. As you may have guessed, we have heard from the Duke."

"Guess I saw the letter written," Gryde responded.

"Quite so; therefore I need not read the same to you. His Grace tells me that he had made your acquaintance in New York, that you intended coming to England for some months, and further that you required a large house for the term. I rather gather that you agreed to take Redburn Castle on the spot."

"Well, I guess I'm a business man," Gryde observed. "And I've heard of the Castle from one who has been a guest there. I made the Duke an offer for six months, and passed the cheque there and then. If I continue for another six months, I am to let you know, and pay the next cheque over to you."

"Absolutely correct," Sutton smiled. "You will like to take possession at once?"

"Just so. In consideration of the amount paid I am to have the run of everything: the cellar, the stables, in fact, the whole show. The staff of servants will remain, but they are to look to you for their wages, you also defraying the expenses of the house, minus legitimate housekeeping. Am I right, Mr.Sutton?"

"Absolutely, my dear sir, absolutely. I will see that you have no trouble this way. And when should you like to take possession?"

"Next Monday, if you can manage matters?"

"Nothing could be easier. I will send one of our staff to Redburn, and he shall explain everything to the steward, and housekeeper. If there is nothing else"

"There is nothing else, and I am wasting your valuable time. Good-day."

Cora thrilled with excitement. Swift has said that every woman is a rake at heart, and Cora possessed a native love for adventure. She knew perfectly well that she would have all the fun of an illicit incident capable of many opportunities without much risk so far as she was concerned. Also she had perfect faith in Gryde. Whatever happened he would see her safely through. Her eyes danced with fun as she met Gryde's gaze.

"It will be splendid," she said. "Paul, what shall we do next?"

"Lunch," Gryde said laconically. "I told the man to drive to Verrey's. In the next few days you will have plenty to do getting your traps ready."

A dainty luncheon was ordered and dispatched. Over the champagne Cora dilated upon the fun and enjoyment she meant to have. Doubtless, the county would call, and for once in her life she could play the great lady.

"I have fallen in love with your scheme, Paul," she said. "What a wonderful man you are!"

"More wonderful than you think," Gryde said with truth.

"Never mind that. There is one thing that puzzles me. Without paying, how did you get the Duke to write that letter?"

"I didn't get him to do it," Gryde smiled.

"Then how did you come to know it was there?"

Gryde smiled again as he refilled his glass. He paused a moment or two before he proceeded to gratify Cora's curiosity.

"These things are always so easy when you know how they are done," he said. "I knew all about that letter for the very good, simple and sufficient reason that I wrote it myself. Some people might call it forgery—we'll say manipulation."

Cora Coventry's sanguine expectations were not doomed to disappointment. The Lyre and The Universe proclaimed to all and sundry that the wealthy American, Cyrus B. Coventry, had taken Redburn Castle for a term, and then proceeded to quarrel, as usual, as to whether Coventry's pile had been made in hogs or oil. On one point they both agreed—that Coventry was both extremely rich and lavishly hospitable. This being accepted on all hands, it became no matter of surprise that the world of the North Riding of Yorkshire called upon the Coventrys.

Naturally, Cora enjoyed herself to the full. Being possessed of both brains and talent, she had no difficulty in passing with the real sovereign ring. Never before had the gates of Redburn Castle been thrown open so widely; never had such lavish hospitality been known. The Coventrys lived en prince—as indeed they might do, seeing that the whole thing was costing practically nothing. Needless to say, the millionaire tenant of Redburn Castle had the most unlimited credit so far as Metropolitan tradesmen were concerned. Then there were the Redburn cellars, gardens, and stables to fall back upon. By the time Christmas arrived, no more popular couple existed in Yorkshire than the Coventrys.

And now the whole county was agog with excitement. As if to crown their stay in the shire of broad acres, invitations for a dance had been sent out broadcast. At least a thousand guests were bidden; the great banqueting hall had been specially decorated for the occasion; a special train was to bring the supper from London. Gryde rather grudged this train; it was the one item of importance that required good money.

"Never mind," Cora laughed; "I don't suppose we have laid out two hundred pounds in cash all the time we have been here. Upon my word, when I look at the wonderful things here—the plate and the pictures—I wonder at your moderation."

Gryde laughed in his turn.

"So do I," he responded grimly. "Anyway, there is time enough for that. What a dramatic thing if the Duke were to turn up this evening."

Cora protested against any such awful suggestion.

"I should find a way out," Gryde said.

"In fact, I am prepared for any emergency. The stage has been set for weeks past."

A large party of guests dined at the Castle, and about ten the rest of the fortunate ones began to arrive. In the grand old hall, as the clock struck twelve, they all sat down to supper. It would have been hard to imagine a more brilliant or artistic spectacle. It will be a long time before Yorkshire ceases to discuss the night of the Coventry dance at Redburn.

A veritable picture in black lace and diamonds, Cora moved amongst her guests. Her mind was far removed from trouble or danger. As she sailed past an excited group standing in the great hall a chance word fell on her ear and held her to the spot. Just for an instant she swayed and would have fallen. Then she took her courage in both hands. The danger was horribly real and tangible.

In the centre of the little group before her stood a brown, grim-faced man in evening dress. There was nothing terrible about him save the fact that his left sleeve, which was empty, was pinned to his coat. Cora's wits were sharpened; she knew without anyone telling her that this was the Duke of Redburn.

"Miss Coventry," said a gay voice, "will you come here? We have a surprise for you."

"Indeed, that is very kind of you," Cora responded with a gaiety wonderful under the circumstances. "I will be with you in one moment."

Like light Cora flew along the corridor towards the smoking-room. Then she literally fell into the arms of the man she was seeking.

"Cora," Gryde exclaimed, "what on earth is the matter?"

"The Duke," Cora whispered; "he is in the ballroom at this moment."

Gryde smiled. No muscle quivered. He betrayed no emotion whatever.

"Is that really so," he said. "Strange how perverse people are. He might have had the good taste to wait till tomorrow. Cora, can I trust you?"

"Where you are in danger," Cora replied.

"The danger is far less than you think, child. Did I not tell you that I had made special preparations for a contingency like this? And in any case, I have specially arranged it that you shall appear to have been an innocent victim. Go back to the Duke and profess to be delighted to see him. As so many of his own personal friends are here, he will not make a scene—indeed, he is far too much of a gentleman for that. The scene will be with me. And when he asks to see me. tell him as naturally as possible that I have been called away for a little time on business, and that he will find me in the small library writing a letter."

Cora nodded. Her faith in the speaker was implicit.

"Very well," she said; "but there will be no violence?"

"O, dear no. I have always, at least nearly always, avoided that kind of thing. Run along, Cora; time is precious now."

As Cora passed along the corridor, Gryde darted upstairs towards his own room. The Duke of Redburn was still standing talking to his friends when Cora came up. There was a flush on her cheeks, a sparkle in her eyes; otherwise she betrayed no fear.

"Can you guess who this is?" a guest asked Cora.

There came a puzzled pucker in the white forehead, then Cora smiled and held out her hand.

"Our landlord, the Duke," she said, cordially. "What a pleasant surprise! And how nice of you to come at such a time, and in so friendly a way!"

Redburn was too astonished to reply. Was the woman mad to carry her audacity to such a length? Otherwise, her acting was superb.

"I am sorry I did not come before," Redburn at length said, grimly.

"Indeed, so am I," Cora replied. "My brother will be delighted to see you."

"And I can assure you, Miss—er—Coventry, the pleasure will be mutual. I have met your brother before, and shall have no difficulty in recognising him. If you will tell me where I am likely to find him, I will"

"O, a little bit of business has detained him," Cora said, innocently. "You will find him at present in the small library, writing a letter. Don't stand on ceremony."

Redburn responded that he would not do anything of the kind. He was still utterly puzzled by Cora's free and engaging manner.

"She's innocent enough," he muttered to himself as he took his way to the library; "anyone can see that from her face. Probably that scoundrel took her in as he did everybody else. It's lucky I got hold of that stray number of The Lyre."

Redburn opened the library door and closed it behind him. At a table sat a man who appeared to be busily engaged over a letter. The envelope, ready directed, was alongside. The Duke saw the same was addressed to Scotland Yard.

"Well, you scoundrel!" he said, "so I have found you out."

A handsome, clean-shaven face was raised to Redburn's.

"I beg your pardon," came the reply; "did you speak, sir?"

Again Redburn paused. This was not Coventry, or indeed anything like him.

"I beg your pardon," he stammered;

"I took you for Coventry. I am the Duke of—"

The writer rose to his feet with a cry.

"So your Grace has come back," he said. "That accounts for Coventry quitting the Castle so hurriedly just now. He must have seen you."

"But who the deuce are you?" Redburn demanded.

"Well, your Grace," was the reply, " I am known here as James Malcolm, Coventry's new secretary, but as a matter of fact I am a detective from Scotland Yard, and at their instigation I obtained this situation. The suggestion was inspired from New York, for the police there fancy Coventry is a man they want. As to that I cannot say—but I do know the man to be a great scoundrel. We had to proceed quietly, you understand. I trust your Grace has not betrayed the truth."

"I have betrayed nothing," Redburn said impatiently. "When I found this thing out, entirely by accident, I turned back as quickly as possible. My idea was to take the rascal red-handed and give him a sound thrashing before the police appeared. Is Miss Coventry as cool and unscrupulous as her brother?"

"Your Grace may make certain of one thing," Malcolm said earnestly.

"Of this swindle Miss Coventry knows nothing. She really believes her brother to be a millionaire. He left England fourteen years ago and until recently she had never seen him. I am immensely sorry for the poor girl."

"Well, I'm glad to hear that," Redburn muttered. "But don't you think we are wasting time here? If the culprit has spotted me there is no further occasion for diplomacy on your part. The great question now is, where is he?"

"And as it happens I can solve the problem," said Malcolm. "He has hidden himself in the old Smugglers' Cave. There is a full tide by this time, and his escape is cut off for the present. Coventry is quite safe till the morning."

"That won't do for me, Mr. Malcolm. Is there a boat down by the cliffs?"

"There is a boat there, as your Grace is aware."

"Then come on. I shan't rest satisfied until I lay my hands on that scoundrel, who has doubtless some cunning scheme on hand. If you'll come with me now, Mr. Malcolm, I'll make it worth your while."

Malcolm rose with alacrity.

"I will do anything your Grace requires," he said. "Shall we go this way so as to avoid any gossip amongst the guests. Fortunately the night is warm. I will row you to the cave. I know that Coventry is unarmed."

The pair passed out into the garden and along the cliffs. There was only one path down there and no cottage for miles. An intense desolation reigned on the sands. A dozen murders might have been committed there with impunity. A boat lay close to the water's edge, for the tide was fast ebbing.

"Coventry must have swum out," Malcolm suggested. "Will your Grace get in? I can easily shove the boat off."

Malcolm pushed off, and steered with the one scull astern rudder fashion. A grey mist lay over the sea, a crescent moon gave a faint, watery light For some time the craft proceeded, but keeping within a hundred yards of the shore.

"Upon my word," Redburn remarked presently, "out of my many adventures lately I have had none stranger than this. Perhaps you can tell me why Coventry prefers to hide in the Smugglers' Cave?"

"The answer is quite easy," Malcolm smiled. "I can assure you that Coventry is a man of infinite resources. You may be certain that he was prepared for this contingency. He has a steam yacht lying off the roads yonder, and a signal at daybreak would mean that a boat has to be sent off. Can you swim?"

Redburn pointed to his left, vacant sleeve with a smile.

"I once attempted to after losing my arm, and nearly paid the penalty of my over-confidence with my life," he said.

"Why do you ask?"

"Because the scull has slipped from my hand, and we are drifting helplessly out to sea with the tide," Malcolm responded. "If you can't leave I must."

To Redburn's intense astonishment Malcolm promptly plunged overboard.

After a time Redburn saw him emerge on the rocks.

"What are you going to do?" shouted the latter.

"Return to the Castle," came the reply, in a voice that caused Redburn to start. "Good-night, your Grace. Fortunately the night is mild and the sea calm, and no doubt you will be picked up in a few hours. You may yell and scream as loud as you like, for nobody is likely to hear you."

"The scoundrel Coventry!" Redburn roared. "If I could only swim!"

"Lucky you can't," Gryde—otherwise Malcolm—said, grimly. "If you had replied in the affirmative I should have been under the painful necessity of putting a bullet through your head. Good-night."

Leaving the Duke foaming with impotent rage Gryde proceeded leisurely up the cliffs towards the Castle. Outside the main windows he halted. In one of them overhead—his dressing-room—was one lighted up. From the casement depended a knotted rope. Gryde swarmed up like a cat.

To strip off and hide his wet clothing was the work of a moment. In less time than one could believe Gryde was serene and calm in the ballroom again. Smiling, yet with a world of anxiety in her eyes, Cora came towards him.

"Where is the Duke?" she asked aloud.

"I regret to say he has gone," Gryde replied. "He did not come to stay; indeed, but for some business matter he would not have been here at all. He bade me to say everything that was polite to his friends."

Cora drew Gryde on one side. Her lips were pale as ashes.

"Paul," she whispered, "Paul, you have not—"

"Redburn is absolutely safe," Gryde responded. "Not so much as a hair of his head has been injured. He is perfectly safe in more senses than one. Meanwhile you can resume the gaiety necessary to the occasion."

The first faint streaks of dawn were in the sky when the last guest departed. Not till then did Cora and Gryde find themselves free to talk.

"I am to speak and you are to listen, said the latter. "Within half an hour I must be clear of this house, child. Never mind how I go and in what guise, because that is my secret. I am going to leave you here, presumably to stand the brunt of the fray, but really to shield you from danger. Understand that you are simply the tool in the hands of a rascally brother. You have been cruelly deceived. On my dressing-table is a letter to you confessing my fault and imploring your forgiveness. A consummate actress like you can carry off the thing perfectly. Besides, you have had a really good time of it, and now you must pay the piper. When Redburn does turn up, your cue is not to know I have really gone. Au revoir."

With a careless wave of his hand, Gryde turned away. A little later a figure stole from the house in the grey of the dawn and disappeared along the cliffs. And it is, perhaps, hardly necessary to say that Cyrus B. Coventry is still at large.

It is hardly necessary either to state that Redburn turned up in due course. Cora received him smilingly. Where was her brother? Why, in bed still. Cora's astonishment to find this a mistake was artistic, her grief when she came to read the fatal letter a study. Redburn, whose nature is sentimental, was profoundly moved at this distress. He blamed himself. Cora he did not doubt for a moment. And when she departed for London later in the day he saw her to the station in his own car. riage. Was there anything he could do?

"Nothing," Cora said faintly. "All I want is to be alone."

Once alone she speedily dried her tears. A queer smile was on her face.

"If I liked," she said to herself, "and if I cared for Paul a little less, it is just possible I might end my life as a respectable humdrum duchess!"

"CRYSOLINE LIMITED"

CHAPTER I

During the last few months no proprietary article had loomed larger on the public eye than the latest and greatest creation, "Crysoline." The powers claimed for this marvellous cure were stupendous. Anything from heart disease to bankruptcy disappeared like magic before one bottle of this sovereign specific, the price of which was a modest twenty-five cents, surely a reasonable figure to pay for a sound body and an equally sound estate?

Nothing of the kind had ever been so intelligently advertised before; no sum was too great to pay the clever "adsmith "—e.g., advertisement maker—for a really novel and striking appeal to the great American nation. In six months the proprietors of "Crysoline" had expended a quarter of a million dollars this way.

Testimonials came pouring in from all parts of the country. So far as sprains, scalds, bruises and the like were concerned, beyond doubt "Crysoline" formed a wonderful remedy. Of the amount of business done there could be no doubt. In a little more than half a year the proprietor had built up a gigantic concern.

So far as it went, Gryde was quite satisfied with his accomplishment. He had purchased the recipe for "Crysoline" for a trifle, really with the object of blinding Cradlestone to the reasons which brought him so near the latter's estate.

A chance conversation, as we know, was responsible for the rest. With the Cradlestone millions at his command, why not push the thing. And then, as the scheme evolved itself in Gryde's busy brain, he saw his way to a coup so great, so certain and remunerative, that he chuckled with delight.

With characteristic dash and energy he threw himself into the new venture. Most men would have been satisfied with the result achieved, but not so Gryde. The predatory instinct prevented anything of the kind.

Meanwhile the pear was ripening; the time was coming when Gryde hoped to lighten the pockets of some of the smartest men in the world, e.g., the Wall Street stockbrokers. Cradlestone chuckled as Gryde hinted at this. He and the latter had met frequently lately, and Cradlestone, whilst bearing no malice, was fully determined to get back his own on the very first opportunity.

Therefore the oil king rubbed his hands and smiled as he read his Sun a few days later. He began to see Gryde's game, or at least so he thought. Gryde, otherwise Manners, was about to turn "Crysoline" into a limited liability company. This would bring the owner of the latest nostrum in direct communication with Wall Street, and it would go hard indeed, Cradlestone thought, if, with others, he could not squeeze Manners dry.

"Those smart fellows always overreach themselves," he said. "That man had better have kept to trade. Within three months he will be stripped of the last feather. I'll get some of my money back, and I'll get 'Crysoline' into the bargain."

And Cradlestone fell to reading the full-paged prospectus of "Crysoline" with new satisfaction. The figures therein contained admitted of no doubt, certified as they were by the leading firm of accountants in New York. From the very first the nostrum seemed to have paid. The sixth month showed a profit of one hundred thousand dollars. Going on the average, the proprietor appeared to be quite justified in the expectation that the profits for the first year would reach one million and a-half dollars. And in asking the public for twenty million dollars, the request seemed reasonable. From New York to San Francisco every paper of note published that advertisement.

The whole of the capital was offered to the public in ten-dollar shares. Cradlestone made a rapid calculation on the margin of his Sun. It seemed to him that by the time the expenses were paid, Gryde's four millions could be exhausted. That Gryde had possessed any capital beyond the amount extracted over the oil venture, Cradlestone did not believe.

"I'll give him a lesson he's likely to remember," said the millionaire.

Needless to say the "Crysoline" boom attracted its fair share of attention. Gryde had not been carefully preparing the ground for nothing. He had paid in the most liberal manner for his advertisement, and he got it all back now in generous puffs. Within a week of the preliminary announcements in the Sun and World, the whole of the capital had been subscribed. Cradlestone chuckled.

True, Gryde had money again to carry on the war. But only ten per cent of the capital was paid on allotment, and no further call, according to the conditions, could be made before the expiration of three months. And in that time many a good ship had been wrecked by the brokers in Wall Street.

Of the plot against him Gryde appeared to know nothing. He applied cheerfully for a Stock Exchange quotation and got it as a matter of course. For the first two or three days "Crysoline" shares were at a premium, little business being done. It was at this point that Cradlestone began to act.

Not that he intended to operate direct himself. He was quite prepared to risk a million or two. Risk! There was none; the thing was a certainty.

Cradlestone's confederates were one of the biggest firms on the market. The mere fact of their buying or selling anything usually sufficed to make or mar the stock. And Cradlestone displayed most unusual candour in the matter.

With his feet on the table and a green cigar in the corner of his mouth, he declared his plans to Alnor Bly, head of the firm of Bly, Sulley and Bly.

"I'm going to bear that stock," he said. "I've bought a big block already at a premium—a couple of million dollars worth, I suppose. By-and-bye there'll be some queer rumours on the market as regards 'Crysoline.'"

"All the same, I wish it was mine," Bly remarked sententiously.

"As a matter of fact, so do I," Cradlestone replied. "It's a good thing—one of the best things offered to the public for many a year. But I owe Manners a grudge, and I mean to pay him off and put money in my pocket at the same time."

Bly nodded. He began to see his patron's drift.

"I think I understand," he said. "You want the concern for yourself."

"Yes; and I mean to have it, too. If you manipulate matters properly you'll find it worth your while. What you have to do is this: take a third of my stock and offer it at ten per cent discount. That will cause a big slump, and frighten all the little men. I'll see that the papers are fed with sensational paragraphs. Once the thing is started others will follow, and before anyone knows what has happened we'll have 'Crysoline' down to ten cents. Some fool is certain to start legal proceedings, and that will settle it."

"Quite so. And then, Mr. Cradlestone?"

The millionaire winked from behind the pungent cloud of his cigar.

"Then it will be time to buy," he said. "The bottom will be knocked out of Manners by that time, and all we have to do is to step in and pick up the pieces. There's nothing new or original about the business; but one thing is certain: if the thing does come off, I shall have a veritable gold-mine."

Bly was quite of the same opinion. He was of opinion privately that he meant to have a finger in the pie also. It was not usual for Cradlestone to be so communicative. Nor did he deem it necessary to explain that his very candour was intended to draw Bly into the venture, and ensure a still further depreciation.

"They'll all tumble to it," said Bly.

"Let them," Cradlestone replied. "So much the better for us. They won't know when the pear is ripe for buying, and we shall. So long as they help us to bear the stock down we can sit quiet and make use of 'em."

This interesting conversation found its way in due course to the ears of Felix Gryde. He had not the slightest objection to pay for information of this kind, and the clerk who had listened returned to his desk well satisfied with his hour's work.

Not that there was any news conveyed to Gryde. He knew perfectly well what line of action Cradlestone would take, but all the same it was just as well to be perfectly sure. Cradlestone's scheme was a very pretty one, but it lacked originality, which was where Gryde had the advantage of him. The average man would have abandoned the game at once and sued for terms, but then Gryde was by no means an average man.

"I always like to help anyone when I can," he muttered, "and I am going to help Cradlestone to knock those shares down. Perhaps he would sing a different tune if he knew how many I hold under different names. And if his soul yearns for paragraphs detrimental to the company and my humble self, he shall have enough and to spare."

The next day the campaign began in earnest. By, closing time, "Crysolines" had declined ten points. The financial scribes were gloomy and mysterious. Private holders began to be alarmed. And the following morning "Crysolines" declined with a rush. Some four millions of stock were on the market, and by afternoon they could be had for any price.

Cradlestone watched the proceedings with feelings of satisfaction. Four millions of his dollars had been absolutely thrown away, but still he smiled.

He knew perfectly well that those millions would come back after many days swollen and multiplied like a mountain stream after a snowstorm.

Before the end of the week the rout of "Crysoline" was complete. Cradlestone's prophecy that the shares would be down to ten cents was verified to the letter. Angry shareholders wrote epistles to the papers, a score of legal actions were commenced, and absolute ruin seemed to stare Gryde in the face.

And yet as the shares were shot into the market at any price they were bought. Small speculators can always be found at such tempting prices, whilst the general sale still continued, and ten times as many "Crysolines" as could be found were disposed of by brokers who would have to find them at a price a fortnight hence. Cradlestone felt quite satisfied at length.

"Nothing could be better," he said.

"By the time that the fortnightly settlement comes the game will be up, and then we can gradually gather the stock in at our own price. The little holders will only be too glad to sell at a profit."

"There's one difficulty in the way," said Bly. "I've sold far more than we've got. If buyers insist upon a delivery we're in a fix."

"But they won't," Cradlestone said confidently. "We'll offer them a few cents premium, which after all is the thing they require. Within a month 'Crysoline' will be mine, stock, lock and barrel. It will be a nice little lesson to Manners."

But Manners, otherwise Gryde, did not seem to resent the way in which he had been treated. For the present he was, perhaps, the most prominent and worst abused individual in the United States. Nothing was too bad to say about him. He had floated a bogus company, he had placed millions of dollars in his pocket, he had not cared what became of the shares so that he got his plunder. Wall Street had found him out, and in rejecting the fraudulent company had done a service to the State. Whether or not the proprietor of "Crysoline" was to be prosecuted was an interesting problem.

But Gryde took it all smilingly. He even shook hands quite heartily with Cradlestone that afternoon as he and the latter met at Delmonico's at lunch.

"Well," said the millionaire, "and how do you like Wall Street?"

"I have no fault to find with Wall Street," Gryde responded. "The air is bracing and the work there of a variable nature. What I like about the people is that they cling together so. When they start out to ruin a man they do it effectually."

Cradlestcne chuckled. He was in a position to appreciate this humour.

"You are alluding to 'Crysoline,'" he said. "Did I not warn you to keep clear of the Street. Upon my word, you have made a nice mess of it."

"And you are going to pocket a fortune," Gryde replied quite pleasantly. "I know exactly what has happened and who to thank for the present state of affairs."

Cradlestone smiled again.

"You couldn't expect to get the best of me twice," he said. "And I'd give a trifle to know how you managed that oil business."

Gryde denied that there had been any trickery in the business, a mere figure of speech, knowing quite well that the other did not believe him.

"All right," Cradlestone laughed, "but you are a good fighter, and I shouldn't wonder if you picked it all up again, yet. But not in 'Crysoline'—you can regard that as gone."

Gryde rose, buttoning his gloves slowly.

"There's many a slip, you know," he said, "and you are not safe till after settling day. You may not be the only one in the swindle. You object to the term? Very well, we will say the financial transaction. We shall meet again."

"Often, I trust," said Cradlestone. Gryde muttered something in reply and strode from the room.

CHAPTER II

Cradlestone strode into Bly's office with the inevitable green cigar in the corner of his mouth. Settling day had arrived, a day which was intended to be a kind of financial Waterloo. All the same, Bly's face was more befitting Bonaparte than that of Wellington.

"Anything wrong?" Cradlestone asked as he dropped into a chair.

"Hang me if I know," Bly replied.

"I've got a letter here that puzzles me. Read it."

Bly tossed the letter across the table, and Cradlestone read as follows:—

Lexington Avenue,
July 18th, 18—.

DEAR SIR,—

We hold contract notes of yours whereby you are pledged to deliver to our client some hundred thousand odd shares in Crysoline, Limited. We enclose list of prices at which the same were purchased from day to day and the prices of the same. We shall be glad to complete the delivery in the course of the day.

Faithfully,
MORGAN AND CO.

Cradlestone knitted his brows over this document. He could not make it out at all.

"It seems to me," he said presently, "that somebody must have got wind of my intentions. We may have to share the plunder after all. You must arrange terms."

"But I have three other letters to precisely the same effect," Bly proceeded. "You see the position. I sold all the shares you had at par, so there is no loss. Then we offered thousands of shares according to your instructions at a few cents. Somebody else is having a flutter at the same game, and we shall have to deliver."

"Then you must go out and buy for the purpose," said Cradlestone. "In fact, you had better start buying all you can lay your hands on. We must be in a position to satisfy these people at the price they purchased at before we can do anything for ourselves. Then you must slip in and scoop the market."

"The price is certain to rise directly we do."

"Of course, I am prepared for that. So long as I can buy the bulk of the shares practically at my own price, I don't care. You get off down to the Street. I'll drop in and see you again directly after lunch."

When Cradlestone returned, whistling serenely, he found Bly sitting with a white face before his desk. An empty champagne bottle was by his side.

"Dyspeptic," the millionaire suggested. "Ah, I can feel for you!"

"I guess you'll feel for yourself, too, when you hear what I have to say," Bly groaned. "By four o'clock you and I between us have to deliver over a million shares in 'Crysoline.' Actually, we don't possess a fifth of them. And there isn't a share to be got at any price."

"Not a share to be got! It's only a matter of money."

"Money has nothing whatever to do with it. Ah, there are others in the soup besides ourselves—others who have sold and can't find the paper. I've seen practically every broker in the market, and not one of them has a sheet of scrip. Since morning 'Crysolines' have gone up from ten cents to a point over three dollars."

Cradlestone groaned. If this was so, a fearful loss awaited him. To put it plainly, he had sold thousands of shares at ten cents, shares which he did not. possess, and now he was called upon to produce for three dollars what he had to surrender for about a tenth of that amount.

"Then who in the name of Fate has the shares?" he asked.

"That is the mystery," said Bly; "I don't know."

Cradlestone was silent. He had never for a moment anticipated anything like this. Was it possible, he wondered, to get hold of bona fide shareholders and—but no. The thing must be carried over till the next settlement, and meanwhile some means might be found whereby the dark operation could be squeezed.

"Of course we must carry over," said Bly.

"Of course, and meanwhile you had better see Morgan."

In the end Bly and Cradlestone saw Morgan and Co. together. The latter received them with a twinkle in his eye. He listened to all they had to say.

"Carry over if you like," he said, "still, I'd settle if I were you."

"Confound you!" Cradlestone cried impatiently; "you know perfectly well that we have not the shares to deliver."

"Perfectly," was the cool response, "but I have, and you can have them at a price."

"And what is your price."

"Face value, ten dollars; and I can supply as many as you want. O, I know quite well what you are going to say. The market price is only three dollars. But it might as well be three millions as far as you are concerned, because you can't deliver. But you'll have to pay more than three dollars this day fortnight."

All the same Cradlestone proposed to carry over till next settling day. He still hoped to find a way to circumvent the dark speculator. A meeting was held of those likely to be victims, and a bold attempt to knock "Crysoline" out of the market was resolved upon. The next day a big block of stock was offered at eight cents. Almost before the offer was made, the whole lot were taken by Morgan and Co. The conspirators decided that this kind of policy was a mere sinful waste of good money. So "Crysoline" stood firm at three dollars, and when the next settling day arrived the murder was out.

A defeated band of victims gathered in the offices of Morgan and Co., with terms. They would pay two and a-half dollars in settlement of all claims, which surely ought to satisfy Morgan's client, who had practically bought at ten cents.

"I'm very sorry, gentlemen," Morgan replied, "but I cannot possibly accept your offer without consulting my client. Perhaps you would like to see him."

Without exception the victims of cunning machinations thought they would. And when, a few minutes later, Gryde, otherwise Manners, stepped into the office, a groan went up. They were trapped beyond hope of escape.

"You wished to see me, gentlemen," Gryde said pleasantly. "Can I do anything for you?"

By common consent Cradlestone was pushed forward as spokesman.

"To tell you the truth," he said, "I rather expected this. I suppose you know that you have got the lot of us in a very tight place."

"Yes," Gryde said grimly. "I've got you where you thought to have me."

"Quite so, quite so. The question is, what will you take to settle?"

"It isn't a question of settling at all," Gryde responded. "Every share that came on the market fell into my hands. It did not take me long to see Mr. Cradlestone's game. I bought these shares in good faith; you contracted to deliver them at prices from three dollars to ten cents—"

"Mostly the latter," Cradlestone groaned.

"So much the better for me. All I want are my shares!"

"But we haven't got them," Cradlestone cried.

"I know it. All the same you are legally bound to deliver them. If you sell what you haven't got it is nothing to me. Your game was to break me down, and you failed. Will you be so good as to deliver me my shares."

"Man alive," Cradlestone yelled, "where are we to get them?"

"From me, seeing that I actually possess the lot."

"At three dollars, of course, Mr. Manners?"

"Not much," Gryde said drily. "I am ready to place you in a position to carry out your lawful obligations at the price paid by the public—ten dollars."

Then followed an awkward silence. Gryde was in a position to sell for ten dollars what, a few minutes later, would be handed back to him for some paltry cents. The thing spelt ruin to more than one man there."

"This is nothing less than a deliberate swindle," Cradlestone cried passionately.

"Call it what you please," Gryde responded as coolly. "I have my rights, and I fully intend to stand by them. As soon as I saw what was going to happen, I took measures accordingly. A deliberate plan was laid to ruin me, and, instead of making a fuss, I set to work to devise some means of giving you clever gentlemen a lesson. When I realised that you were all recklessly selling what you hadn't got, I saw my way. All the shares were offered to the public, but I took good care to keep them for the most part in my own hands. As you sold, so I bought; and if I liked to ask you a million dollars per share for delivery, you would have to accept it or get broken. I could force every man of you into bankruptcy if I liked: I could pull Wall Street about your ears. And I should be none the worse off, because, you see, all this time I've got the shares."

There was no denying this pregnant statement. Gryde was in a position to throttle every man there. All they could do was to make terms.

"We throw ourselves on your mercy," Cradlestone said at length. "Let us have the lowest price you will accept for your shares?"

"Ten dollars a share," Gryde snapped; "not a cent less."

"You will give us time to carry over till next settlement, so as to discuss it?"

"Certainly I will. If the markets go up the ten dollars go up, too."

The deputation withdrew fuming. There was wailing and gnashing of teeth in Wall Street, but all the tears were in vain. And the storm broke out afresh when the deputation came to meet the master of the situation once more.

"We'll pay the ten dollars," said Cradlestone.

"Fifteen dollars," Gryde said, suavely.

"The market has gone up. I warned you that, if such were the case, I should have to charge the difference. And that is the price to which I sold a batch to an investor yesterday."

"You're not in earnest," Bly faltered.

"Gentlemen," Gryde responded, in tones of steel, "I never was more serious in my life. This is a case of diamond cut diamond, and my diamond is the harder of the two. And if I carry over again the price will be twenty dollars. The longer you fight the thing off the worse will it be for you."

Cradlestone threw up his hands with a gesture of despair.

"Six millions of dollars!" he yelled, "clean robbed of six millions! If I had only known when I had you out yonder, I would have shot you like a dog. A bullet or a partnership I'd like to present you with—and I shouldn't care which."

"I am infinitely obliged to you," Gryde responded. "I may say that is the finest compliment I ever had paid me in my life."

Hardly had the blackest of black Mondays passed away, and the pungent newspaper chaff at the expense of Wall Street died away, ere New York had another sensation connected with the same "Crysoline, Limited." Fires in the capital city of America are not few and far between, but the town had not for some time past enjoyed such a blaze as that afforded by the palatial premises of the above company. No sooner had the citizens generally devoured the six lines of brevier and two columns of cross heading describing the event when the evening papers came out with the climax. And this is what the Evening Sun had to say on the matter:—

LAST NIGHT'S BIG, BAD BLAZE
THE END OF A NEW MILLIONAIRE'S SHORT BUT BRILLIANT CAREER
MANNERS THE MAGNIFICENT PERISHES IN THE FLAMES

He slept on the premises last night, because of anonymous letters threatening to destroy the block, which, by the way, was heavily insured. Manners laughed at the letters, and promised the incendiaries a warm reception. But got one himself. Caretakers are unanimous on this point. Still, the body has not been found. Nor, under the circumstances, is it likely to be. Full details.

We regret to say that Mr. Manners was on the burnt-out premises last night, and that he perished in the flames. No blame is attached to anyone, nor do the police credit the suggestion that the fire was inspired. As to the rest, nothing can be known till Manners' representatives in England have been communicated with. The absence of anybody to bury will be regretted in Wall Street; otherwise the financial gang would assuredly attend the funeral.

Gryde read the above on the deck of the Campagnia, then creeping out of dock. Under the circumstances, he had deemed it better to disappear in that way. He had become so great a man that an ordinary exit was impossible. Gryde mused over the matter as he tranquilly smoked a cigar.

"Upon my word," he muttered, "it is remarkably easy to be a millionaire if one only goes about it the proper way. And people are so easily gulled that my life is getting quite monotonous. I've a great mind to retire from the business altogether, and when I have finished off the other little schemes, I will."

CHAPTER I

Gryde was dining the Accredited Agent-General of the State of Mineria at his club. Here Felix Gryde was known as Count Dumaresque, a South American grandee of wealth recently settled in England. For the most part, he surrounded himself with a halo of frosty politeness, which served to keep his fellows at a distance, and prevented the asking of questions. For the rest, he was lean and brown; his buttonhole flaunted the ribbon of some foreign Order.

The Minerian representative was also lean and brown, with a furtive eye and a reputation for dubious veracity. His life was one long battle with the capitalists who regarded Minerian Bonds dubiously. But a liar at once so picturesque and audacious as Don Marcos did not live in vain. At the present moment some twenty millions of British capital were buried in the pocket State, and, like a financial Oliver Twist, Don Marcos asked for more.

In desperate need of five millions, he asked for ten, and consequently got two. Things were very bad in the City, and "dilly-dally duck" cared nothing for the Minerian salt Marcos desired to put on his tail. And this was all the more annoying because Mineria was on the verge of war with the neighbouring "State" of Catagonia over that turtle-fishing business.

Marcos was in despair. His finest romantic flights were spent in Lombard Street in vain. An expert in gold mining had worked at his samples of the precious ore and asked if they had come via the Cape.

"Over the walnuts and the wine" Marcos became expansive. Count Dumaresque, his fellow-countryman, was duly sympathetic. And the latter betrayed such an astounding knowledge of the tortuous ways of Minerian finance as rendered Don Marcos uneasy.

"I declare I am afraid of you," he muttered.

Dumaresque smiled in the most reassuring manner.

"Positively there is no need," he replied. "I have no need to love my country, as you would say if you knew my story; but as she laid down my fortune for me I am not ungrateful, and I hate the Catagonians."

Marcos started. Really, this wonderful man knew everything.

"You are aware we are at loggerheads there?" he suggested.

"Dear friend, you will be at one another's throats ere two months are past," said Dumaresque, with a wave of his cigarette. "Under existing circumstances the prospect frightens you."

"Another million and I should feel easy enough. We want—"

"A line-of-battle ship," Dumaresque put in. "One big armed cruiser to blockade Inique and you would settle the business in a month."

"Parbleu, a wonderful man," Marcos muttered. "Your Excellency has guessed it."

"That is because I have studied the question," said Dumaresque. "A cruiser such as you require would, fully equipped, cost a million. The manning is of no great consequence, nor the officering either for the matter of that. Good men with an eye to ultimate income will flock round you as a matter of course. What could you put down in cash for a ship such as you require?"

"I took £200,000 with me to Belfast and offered to secure the rest," Marcos responded, almost tearfully, "and they laughed politely in my beard."

Dumaresque lent across the table and dropped his voice to a whisper.

"If I provide you with one of the finest line-of-battle ships afloat," he said, "will you hand over the sum in question to me?"

Marcos smiled; and yet Dumaresque's face was grave enough.

"My noble friend is pleased to jest," Marcos muttered.

"Your noble friend was never more serious in his life," came the response.

"You have heard of that new man-o'-war, the Eastern Empress?" The listener's eyes sparkled at the mere suggestion. The Eastern Empress, recently launched from Belfast, was the finest belted cruiser afloat. Her triple-expansion engines were wonders, those quick-firing guns were an army corps in themselves, goodness knows what was the resisting power of the armour-plating; whilst on the trial trip even the boiler tubes had failed to leak, which fact in itself marked a new departure in naval engineering.

"Ah, if we only had a ship like that!" Marcos sighed.

Dumaresque's reply was brief but thrilling.

"Guarantee to hand me over £200,000 at the time I may demand it," he said, "and within two months the Eastern Empress shall be lying in the mouth of your de la Guarde river to do as you please with."

Marcos hastily swallowed another glass of claret. Such an audacious proposal came as a shock to the nerve centres

"I presume you do not mean to insult me?" he gasped.

"You allude to your sense of honour, doubtless," Dumaresque sneered.

"Bah! the sense I mean is my common sense," Marcos responded promptly. "Such a thing could not be done. Even if it were possible detection could speedily follow. Otherwise, the £200,000 is your own."

"It has been as good as my own for some time," said Dumaresque. "The thing is easy as easy—when you know how it is done. What my plans are and whence I derived all my information is my own secret. Within three months, two months, the Eastern Empress shall be at the mouth of de la Guarde. The spot is desolate; there is a good natural harbour there, and with your own engineers specially imported with the necessary appliances to the spot, a few days will alter the Eastern Empress beyond recognition. Then you can boldly sail into your chief harbour of San Maza and make up your complement of men and officers."

"Still, there are lions in the path," Marcos suggested. "Where did the ship come from?"

"Let a paragraph go round the papers that an American firm has turned out the cruiser for you. Do this at once. Mention a well-known firm by name— and if it is only for the sake of the advertisement they will never contradict the report."

Marcos wagged his head sagely.

"My faith, but you are a wonderful man!" he said. "O, yes; you shall do as you like, all the more as I run no risk in the matter. Still, there remains one lion, the biggest of the lot. The British lion, what of him?"

"You mean there will be a fuss over the loss of the ship?" Dumaresque smiled in the orthodox Mephistophelian manner. "My friend, there will be no fuss whatever. For months I have laid my plans, and they are absolutely flawless. How the thing is to be managed is my secret for the present. I give you my word that there will be no fuss or bother whatever."

"And as to the rest?"

"As to the rest, two months from to-day you will be at de la Guarde with your engineers and workmen. To the hour I shall steam into the harbour. You will come aboard and pay me the £200,000 and provide me with a coaster to take me to San Maza. Is that so?"

Marcos stretched out a lean brown claw eagerly.

"Shake hands upon it," he gurgled. "Providence must have brought us together."

Dumaresque, otherwise Gryde, smiled.

"Heaven helps those who help themselves," he said sotto voce.

CHAPTER II

Gryde's audacious scheme was by no means the inspiration of a moment. Neither could the main idea be termed altogether novel, since the stealing of barks and luggers has ever been a favourite theme of nautical writers. But the spiriting away of a line-of-battle ship at the end of the nineteenth century was quite another matter. Like Mark Twain's "Stolen White Elephant," the affair was certain to cause an immense sensation, for big cruisers, unlike big diamonds, cannot be hidden away in a waistcoat pocket.

Under ordinary circumstances, the recovery of the Eastern Empress was a certainty. True, this could have mattered little to Gryde, provided he got his money, but at the same time he was too finished an artist in crime to leave a thing to chance in this clumsy way. There had to be exceptions, of course, but he preferred the crime that on the surface appeared no crime at all.

In this case there was to be no sensation. This statement seems absurd on the face of it, but nevertheless Gryde had found a way.

Needless to say, the scheme had entailed a considerable expenditure of time and money, Gryde holding with Walpole that the latter commodity will do anything. Certainly it had unlocked certain of the minor secrets of the Admiralty. For instance, the golden key supplied the information that some little friction had arisen between this country und Spain as to the pearl-fishing rights in the Eastralian Ocean, where, strange to say, Mineria and Catagonia bordered. It was an open secret also that the first commission of the Eastern Empress would be for two years in these same waters. This step was intended to serve a dual purpose—to prove to Spain that no nonsense would be entertained, and also to revise the Admiralty charts, which were acknowledged to be defective so far as certain parts of the Eastralian Ocean were concerned.

Gryde's movements were carefully arranged. All that the Admiralty were doing in the matter he knew perfectly well. He knew, for instance, that the First Lord and the commander of the Eastern Empress were discussing certain important matters late on the night following his meeting with Marcos, long after the First Lord's household had gone to bed. Gryde had oral and ocular demonstration of this fact, and he stood outside Sir Dorian Bax's library door in his stocking feet listening to the palaver. This act of burglary was necessary, as will hereafter appear.

A scent of fresh tobacco smoke floated out from the library. Gryde wondered if he might indulge himself, then he abandoned the suggestion. The mixture of pleasure and business rarely leads to satisfactory results.

To overhear and oversee this interview Gryde had remained perdu in the Grosvenor Crescent house for two hours. Through the half-opened door he could see Lord Ararat and Captain James Clinton carefully studying a huge chart laid out before them on the table.

"Not altogether satisfactory," said his lordship.

"Well, no," Clinton admitted. "The fact is we want a new survey of this portion of the Eastralian Seas. This Mineria-Catagonia business will be a fine excuse for sounding The Gut without arousing the suspicion of anybody. We are there to protect English interests in case of trouble."

Captain Clinton smiled, and the First Lord smiled also. An eminent cotton-spinner who had made a fortune, and attained a peerage, was just the very man for an enlightened Government to choose as head of the Admiralty. Lord Ararat was profoundly ignorant of everything appertaining to his office, and did no worse for the fact.

"Dangerous place, The Gut, isn't it?" he asked.

Clinton replied in the affirmative. Still, the chart lying on the table there was a reliable one, with all the dangerous rocks and shoals marked upon it. The same had been recently purchased from a scientific Catagonian with a bent for turning his knowledge to account.

"The only place we have to fear," Clinton concluded, "is the Hen and Chickens reef. The currents there are extremely dangerous. Still, with a chart like this, I fail to see how we can get into trouble. My intention is to go entirely by the chart, taking fresh soundings by the way. In two years the whole thing should be complete."

"You are taking a scientific survey party along?"

"Yes, four of them altogether. Mr. Erenthal is an exceedingly clever German, and his friends are all enthusiasts, I'm told. The thing is somewhat irregular, but I've no doubt we shall find these gentlemen of great assistance."

The listening Gryde smiled. A little while later and he would be playing the part of the distinguished German savant about to become a guest on the Eastern Empress in the cause of science. As to the others, they are merely accomplices to be used and discarded at leisure.

Lord Ararat yawned, and looked somewhat pointedly at his watch. The hour was late, and his lordship had been to many functions the same evening. Clinton rose.

"I will not detain you any longer," he said.

"Well, I am tired," the First Lord confessed. "Leave this chart with me till to-morrow; I will show it to Cansford as arranged. You shall have it back before you leave for Portsmouth on Saturday. Good-night."

Clinton took another cigarette and departed. Then the First Lord proceeded to fasten up the house and creep yawningly to bed, having first dropped the Eastralian chart into a drawer under the library table.

Half an hour later Gryde sat at the same piece of furniture carefully examining the chart with the aid of a shaded candle. The chart he compared minutely with several scraps of paper which he produced from his pocket. Then, with a pair of compasses and an ivory scale, he went over the glazed cloth. From his pocket he produced a tiny phial and a camel's-hair pencil. A few strokes with the latter, charged with some of the liquid from the phial, left every portion touched blank. A box of water-colours were next brought into use, and then an hour's careful work followed. The alterations made were so skilful as to defy detection, but they were ample for Gryde's purpose.

Once dry the chart was replaced in the drawer, and for the present Gryde's task was at an end. A few minutes later he stood in the deserted street.

"A pity to leave the door unfastened," he muttered, "because those little things are inartistic. Not that the servants will notice: they will merely conclude that their master came in late and forgot to lock up. And I can safely indulge in a smoke now."

Gryde strolled along the street to his lodgings in an amiable frame of mind; all his plans were complete and success semed assured. The alterations made in the chart were mere pin points by comparison, but then an inch thereon meant miles of blue water. The work of a few moments was the result of months of steady toil and study. If genius be an infinite capacity for taking pains, then veritably Gryde was a genius in his way.

Two days later Gryde started for Portsmouth to take his place on the Eastern Empress. He was altered out of recognition. He had a rotund figure, a profusion of fair hair, and his eyes looked out from rimmed spectacles. In the gaze of the world he was no longer Felix Gryde, but Herr Max Erenthal.

The latest and most expensive addition to Her Majesty's Navy had been at sea now for some six weeks. The Eastern Empress had exceeded the same sanguine estimate formed of her character, and Captain Clinton was serene in the knowledge that he commanded the finest ironclad afloat.

It was a perfect October night, summer in those favoured seas where the breeze came cool and crisp, yet laden with spices and perfumes from the group of islands that fringed the mainland of Mineria, hard against the coastline at the end of which lay the harbour of San Maza. Millions of stars flamed in the deep blue of the arch; on the water lay an arc of lights, the meaning of which those upon the Eastern Empress knew perfectly well. They were Catagonian gunboats watching San Maza as a cat watches a mouse.

Clinton, with some of his officers about him, was smoking a cigar on the quarter-deck. Amongst the group was Herr Erenthal. His subordinates were somewhere down in the engine-rooms. Being of a mechanical turn of mind they haunted the engineers.

"Why don't those beggars fight?" Clinton asked. "Those gunboats are enough in themselves to force a declaration of war."

"They wait for their new ship from America, these Minerians," Erenthal smiled. "When she come you will see what you call ructions. And I shall like to see der fun. One gets tired mit all dese dredging and sounding."

"You can take the steam pinnace and go ashore if you like," said Clinton.

Erenthal expressed his thanks. He was just going to ask the same favour, he said. An hour later he was waddling across the quay-head at San Maza looking about him as if quite uncertain of his direction, and yet at the same time there seemed to be a deal of method in his drifting. Quite naturally he found himself at length in a café, and as if the thing were the merest accident in the world, who should be there but Marcos.

"A fine night, my friend," said the latter.

"Fine indeed," Gryde responded. "But you would not have recognised me had I not given you what some people call the office. You have seen the ship?"

"Ay, indeed. If she were only ours! Those gunboats! Well, if you are successful we will make short work of them."

"I am always successful," Gryde said calmly. "Three days from now the Eastern Empress will sail into de la Guarde. All your men are ready?"

"They are now waiting with all appliances."

"Good. I leave it to your people to alter the Eastern Empress beyond recognition. The thing is nothing like so difficult as it would appear. There is another thing to which I would direct your earnest attention. About the same time that my prize arrives at de la Guarde the complement of an English man-o'-war will reach San Maza—in boats. They must be got away at once: plead the disturbed state of the country or what you will. Because, if they should happen to be still there when your fine cruiser arrives—"

And Gryde paused significantly. Marcos nodded.

"I am obliged to you," he said; "it shall be done. "Is there any more?"

"A little thing—a mere trifle," Gryde replied. "When you board the Eastern Empress and hand me over that money, you will find my four accomplices on board. Whilst I go on to San Maza with the coaster you have for me, they will remain to enjoy your hospitality for a day or two. If anything happens to them in the meantime I will try and put up with the loss with fortitude."

"Dead men tell no tales," Marcos whispered.

"I never heard of one who did," Gryde said drily; "neither do they ever cause trouble as to their share of the plunder."

The two men exchanged significant glances and Gryde rose from his seat. He lapsed quite naturally into his rolling gait again; he looked the amiable absent-minded savant to the life. San Maza was a charming place, he informed Captain Clinton a little time later.

"Sorry not to have seen it," said the latter.

"Perhaps you may yet," Gryde smiled. "One never can tell. Pouf, I must now to my cabin to write up those soundings. I wonder where my fellows are."

As it happened the confederates were in the cabin awaiting the chief. As he closed the door they looked towards him eagerly.

"You have news for us," one of them asked.

"Yes, I have news," Gryde whispered. "I have at length all the information about the tides that I require. An intelligent native yonder told me everything. On Wednesday night at ten we shall be on the edge of the Hen and Chickens reef. I have arranged all that very nicely with the Captain. There will be no moon, and it will be pitch dark for some hours afterwards. At eleven o'clock on the night in question you will all be at your posts down below. There will be no need for me to give you the signal, you will feel it. If all goes well, a few hours later will see you worth £10,000 apiece."

The listeners smiled: the prospect was an exceedingly pleasant one.

"It all depends upon you now," Gryde proceeded. "The ship is steering by the chart, as these people think, a degree or so to the south of the reef. As you know perfectly well, we are steering right on to it. When you feel the first shock, you will know exactly what to do. That water balance must be shifted as arranged to convey the idea that the vessel is filling, and thus increase the confusion. This course will also lighten the ship by the head, and enable her to float."

"Yes, but will she float?" a listener asked.

"Naturally. The reef we shall strike upon will be the softest coral, and we shall run aground at dead low water. An hour later and we shall be off. By this time the ship's complement will have taken to the boats, and we shall be left on board. With fair weather, it's hard if four practical engineers like you cannot navigate this boat the hundred odd miles to de la Guarde. And long before daylight the ship's crew will be hull down behind the horizon."

With perfect confidence in his scheme, and his ability to carry it out, Gryde dismissed his confederates, and retired to rest. Next morning showed the coast of Mineria, a faint blue streak upon the weather bow, and the whole of that day Gryde was busy with her soundings.

The succeeding day worked slowly out, and night fell at length like a black cloud out of nothingness. Till nearly ten o'clock Gryde was busy in his cabin, and then he crept up on deck, as if desiring not to be noticed.

His gait had lost its roll, his step was lithe and elastic as that of a cat. He crept from place to place, avoiding the lanes of light left by the ship's lanterns, and crouching in the shadows.

Presently he gained the coign of vantage he required—the shadow of the wheel-house. A calm and balmy night, with a clear seaboard, the watch were half sleeping on the deck. Not a single officer was to be seen. Gryde peeped at his watch, and saw that the hour had come.

Where the Eastern Empress was on that placid sea he knew to an inch, and the knowledge was not without its meed of anxiety. The ship was listing away a little to the south; a space longer, and the reef would be missed. The carelessness or ignorance of the steersman was wrecking Gryde's plans.

He shut his teeth close together. Like a shadow he slid into the wheel-house. Something long and bright came from his pocket: it flashed high in the air, and then crashed at some soft substance.

Pierced to the heart by the unerring sweep of Gryde's blade, the steersman collapsed upon the floor with one long sigh, and then all was still. The die was cast now; this rash step had become absolutely necessary. Gryde laid his hand upon the powerful yet delicate machinery, and altered the ship's course almost imperceptibly. Still, it was sufficient for his purpose.

"That's the worst of having a lot of fools to deal with," he muttered. "When you have to rely upon anyone else, it always upsets your plans. A risk of this kind should have been absolutely unnecessary."

Cool as he was, Gryde was conscious of the blood singing in his ears. Left alone for five minutes, he knew that he was safe. But already there were steps coming in his direction. It became a mere matter of seconds. Would it become necessary to take a second life, Gryde wondered, and were they never going to strike—

A hand was laid on the door of the wheel-house. Gryde was preparing to spring forward, when the Eastern Empress gave a shiver and groan from end to end like some gigantic creature in mortal agony. Then there followed a tremendous crashing and grinding, and the cruiser was still.

A yell of triumph rose to Gryde's lips, but he suppressed the desire. All the same, it is doubtful as to whether or not it would have been heard, for already hundreds of feet were trampling the decks.

As if to increase the horror of the situation, there followed a loud report from below, and then the sound of water as if pouring ton after ton into the hold of the doomed vessel. Almost immediately she began to sink by the stern.

"Get out the boats!" came the stern command. "Steady there! Plenty of time if you fellows only keep your heads."

Gryde watched everything from the seclusion of the wheel-house. The crew worked as steadily and as orderly as if on parade. In a remarkably short space of time the last boat was lowered and manned.

Gryde and his confederates had the Eastern Empress to themselves. All the same, it was some time before they dared to move, and then one by one the lights were put out and the ship plunged into darkness. Down in the engine-room Gryde found his grimy, perspiring assistants.

"Remarkably well done," he said, approvingly. "That explosion and the rush of water finished the business off dramatically. When the tide rises, the water-ballast will find its way back again quite naturally, and all we shall have to do is to steer by the chart—our chart, of course."

"But will she float?" one of the confederates asked.

"As sure as you will some day be hanged," Gryde responded pleasantly. "Can't you feel her swinging at the bows already? One of you go up to the wheel-house with some sacking and a shot or two. You'll find a body there to dispose of. That fool of a steersman didn't know his business, and I had to— Mind you clear everything up."

Higher and higher rose the tide and more buoyant became the Eastern Empress. Finally, she rose like a thing of life. It was two o'clock before Gryde gave the signal. There was a stern triumph in his eyes.

"Start the engines again," he said curtly. "By noon to-morrow we shall be ready for them off de la Guarde."

Three days later, at about the same time that the news of the total loss of the Eastern Empress reached England, her ship's company, intact save one missing man, were leaving Mineria by a special steamer chartered for them out of courtesy by the Government of the country. The steamer contained one passenger besides, a boasting, inquisitive Yankee, who speedily rendered himself so objectionable as to be tabooed by the rest of the little colony. But the Yankee bore it all philosophically.

"A very good disguise," he told himself, as his cab rolled out of the dock gates a few weeks later. I wonder what those fellows, particularly Clinton, would have said if he'd known the bounder, 'Ezra P. Stanton' and 'Max Erenthal' were one and the same? And I wonder if ever they will discover the trick played upon them? In any case it can't make any difference to me. My dead men will tell no tales."

The Cretan ferment was at its height. Daily did the Chronicle fume and fret, and call upon England to do something. And yet business proceeded as usual, for level-headed men refused to "enthuse" over gallant Greece in her attempt to obtain immortality and Crete at one and the same time.

Still, there were not wanting thousands of people ready to find both money and sympathy for the cause of liberty. And when the Athens correspondent of the Chronicle announced that General Marcos was on his way to England, a gentle thrill of excitement swayed the pulses of the humanitarians.

Marcos' mission was twofold. In the first place, he desired to make clear the Hellenic side of the question, and collect subscriptions for the good cause at the same time. For, beyond all question, the descendants of those famous warriors were very hard up indeed. And Marcos, who had a fine histrionic talent, and some little knowledge of war, hoped to clear some thousands of pounds by the expedition.

It was rather unfortunate that neither the Star nor Chronicle could supply their readers with the photograph of the illustrious warrior who had so suddenly flashed out of nothingness into the concrete form of a celebrity. An urgent wire to Athens was despatched, asking that the void should be filled.

Meanwhile an astute brain was doing its best to supply the deficiency. There was here the material for an adventure, and an opening for ultimate income after Gryde's own heart. He had come along in the hope of something turning up in the near East, and it looked as if he were not to be disappointed.

The newspaper man was up country—at the residence of General Marcos, in fact—when the demand for the photograph came. The American war correspondent, Horace Melville, also formed one of the party. To clear the situation, it would be as well to state that Melville and Gryde were one and the same person. The newspaper man had taken quite a fancy to the jocund American.

"By Jove! I never thought about the photograph," he said. "Marcos is sure to have one. But how to get it to Athens? I can't possibly leave here for a day or two, and then I am going down to the coast when the General's departed."

"I'll go," Melville said promptly. "It's a bit of a risk over those hills alone, but I daresay I shall manage to get through, I've been in Greece so many times."

The disciple of the journalistic-hysterical thanked Melville warmly. Just now his hands were very full indeed, coaching Marcos, whose English was only fair, and further down the coast some English marines had been stealing cockles or some other blazing atrocity.

"You are very good," he said, "and I accept your offer. Perhaps you wouldn't mind posting a batch of copy for me as well. I'll put the photo inside."

Gryde promised to do as desired. It would be a week later, he heard, before Marcos passed by the same road that he was taking to the coast. Then the messenger rode off as if all the furies were pressing close behind him. Not that he proceeded straight to Athens with his native servant; he had a little business to do first. He turned out of the beaten track, and rode far into the hills till night began to fall.

The place where Gryde and his servant Luli pulled rein at length was wild and deserted. High above them towered a range of mountains, fir-covered almost to the summit. There was no sign of life anywhere.

"If this is the spot," said Gryde, "you can give the signal, Luli."

The murderous-looking and none too cleanly Greek placed his fingers to his lips and three times emitted a peculiar whistling scream. Presently there came an answering reply. Two men dropped hand over hand, apparently from the heights, and in a short space of time stood before Gryde and his companion, Nicholi bowed, with the air of one who appreciates his worth. He had the reputation of being the most daring brigand on the peninsula.

"Luli gave you my message, of course," said Gryde. "You know what to do?"

Nicholi nodded, and pulled draughtily at his cigarette.

"Oh, yes," he responded. "I am to make myself master of the General. Also I am to detain him here until I hear from you again; also you are to pay me—"

"Five hundred pounds in good English gold," said Gryde. "Here are the sovereigns. As to the rest, Marcos passes this way on Tuesday. He will have one servant only."

"And my band number seven," Nicholi said, with a smile. "If I remember, your Excellency was to provide me with a pair of American revolvers."

"I have brought them. You fully understand me? The thing is quite simple and easy. As to the rest, Luli will let you hear. I can stay with you no longer; in fact, I must be in Athens by daylight."

When finally Gryde did arrive in Athens, it was alone, for he had rid himself of Luli. And, moreover, he was disguised beyond recognition. He wore the undress uniform of a Greek general, and he looked the character to the life. There was no need to ask any questions, because Gryde knew Athens perfectly well.

Once Gryde had thoroughly rested himself and partaken of food, he proceeded to the modern part of the city, and there entered a photographer's establishment. Needless to say the proprietor was an Englishman, nothing of an up-to-date character like that could have appealed to the Greek native. And there were always plenty of tourists there. The proprietor received Gryde in person, and asked his requirements.

"Well," Gryde responded, "I want my photograph taken. One good cabinet will be sufficient, and I shall require it to-morrow afternoon, properly mounted. I know I am asking a great deal, but I am prepared to pay for the accommodation.

The photographer demurred a little, and finally agreed, as Gryde knew quite well he would. These were the little things that money always procures. The first attempt proved quite successful, and Gryde left the shop with the assurance that the mounted print would be ready for him on the following afternoon.

He was perfectly satisfied with the same when he got it. So far everything had proceeded with the greatest smoothness. Gryde had embarked in more promising ventures, so far as their pecuniary side were concerned, but he could recall nothing that pleased him better than the present undertaking, there was such an element of adventure about it. Gryde smiled as he laid the portrait on the table of his sitting-room. Then he produced the bulky envelope he had promised to forward to the Chronicle office. A little hot water released the flap, and Gryde proceeded to exchange the two photographs, substituting his own for the original, which he carefully destroyed.

"The thing looks like a success," he muttered, "nobody will know but what Marcos is in England; indeed, will they not see his name in the papers? Who would dream that he was close to his own house all the time? And Nicholi will hold him safe, or forfeit the other half of his money. I've only to wait till Tuesday and then—"

Tuesday came in due course, and towards nightfall Gryde strolled out of the city. At a place where the road was deserted he paused before a flat stone lying in the rank grass and flowers. Gryde raised this.

Beneath he found a piece of dirty folded paper. He opened it, and read the pencilled scrawl with more eagerness than usual.

"We have caught the bird," it ran, "and caged him. Nicholi."

Gryde gave a smile of satisfaction.

"The time has come," he said, "the time to act. Positively my last venture looks like being the most fascinating of the lot."

Twenty-four hours later Gryde was steaming towards England.

CHAPTER II

The portrait of General Marcos duly appeared, and for once in a way did not constitute the libel which generally follows on pictorial art in penny daily papers. A glowing biography was attached, the perusal of which caused Gryde to smile, for, sooth to say, his insight into human nature was extensive and peculiar; and, from personal knowledge of Marcos, Gryde would not have written him down either as a hero or philanthropist.

Still, there is always an opening for a lion in London, even though there may be more than a suspicion of clockwork about him, and just for the present the celebrity market was tight. Nansen was elsewhere, and there was nobody to take his place. Moreover, the Greeks had not hitherto forwarded anything like a favourable specimen; and the Cretan question really was occupying a good deal of public attention.

There were some hundreds of thousands of people who were burning with sympathy and full of natural horror of the unspeakable Turk. The morning following "Marcos'" arrival, he held quite a levée in his private room at the Métropole.

Quite a knot of prominent journalists— the kind who write "program"—were there. In their raid they had captured a Duke, a poor thing from a democratic point of view, but quite the most reliable brand in the way of a chairman. The Duke of Clifton, who was young and terribly in earnest, spent most of his time occupying chairs. For the rest, his flagrant socialism was quite a matter of the cuticle.

"We can promise you a grand reception," said the editor of the Telephone; "a strong committee has been formed of which his Grace here is the chairman."

"His Grace is very kind," Gryde said solemnly.

"And we have arranged for a great demonstration in Hyde Park on Sunday!" another journalist put in eagerly.

"We estimate that half a million will be present. It is very fortunate, General, that you have such a command of our tongue."

"You expect me to speak?" Gryde asked. He had overlooked this fact, and to boil up the necessary enthusiasm would be a strain.

"It will be absolutely essential," the Duke remarked; "the very thing we require. You will be able to sway your audience at will."

"And touch their pockets also," Gryde said, with a queer smile. "Shall I confess I came here for that purpose. A poor nation like Greece—"

The Duke hastened to give the desired assurances.

"We have not been idle," he said, "mass meetings are already arranged in all the great towns. Thousands will respond cheerfully to the call. On Sunday you will get an idea what England is like when her ire is roused."

For the first time since the commencement of the present adventure, Gryde began to wish that he had turned his genius in some other channel. It looked as if he was going to be profoundly bored by the whole thing. And if there was one human attribute he disliked more than another it was enthusiasm. Enthusiasm led to all kinds of troubles. All the same, there could be no drawing back now.

The great demonstration duly came off, but the half million of people were conspicuous by their absence. Round the dozen platforms a thin black line gathered, and then finally it came on a pelting storm. Gryde rejoiced from the bottom of his heart.

Nobody appeared to be pleased save the editor of the Telephone. He spoke of the enthusiasm and the crowd, though he was not quite certain that the attendance numbered half a million. He desired to be quite fair, he had no desire to menace the Government unduly as he nobly knocked off an odd fifty thousand.

"All the same," Gryde remarked subsequently, "the thing was an absolute failure. If the North of England only turns out to be the same."

But your real journalist is nothing if not sanguine.

"Wait till you have been to Ironborough," he said.

And after Ironborough, Gryde was fain to confess that things were better than he had anticipated.

The town in question was a great Radical centre; its leading lights were men of wealth, and some six thousand people had gathered for the occasion. At the end of three hours Gryde retired to his hotel the richer by over £4,000. This collection being so large, it was only natural that Coalville, an adjacent and small city, being a city, should desire to go one better. £6,000 odd were collected, and, in the course of a fortnight, Gryde began to feel that he was not living in vain.

An immense concourse of people were packed into the Maryport Town Hall. The Duke of Clifton occupied the chair, and the platform boasted of many a shining light besides. A month had passed, and this was the final meeting in the North, a special effort to wind up a successful tour.

Gryde sat waiting for his turn to speak. He was fairly satisfied, and utterly tired of the whole business. Nearly a hundred thousand pounds had passed into his hands, and he had quite made up his mind, once London was reached, to conveniently disappear. His thoughts were wandering away in the direction of the Southern seas, visions of rest and peace, and sunshine, floated before his eyes.

Then he aroused himself with an effort. Somebody was tugging at his coat-tails. A verbose local actor had just sat down amidst an audible but not too flattering sigh of relief, and Gryde declared that his time had come to speak.

As he lifted himself to his feet a hurricane of cheers burst forth. All he could see was a seething sea of faces as his vision cleared and his senses grew alert. For twenty minutes Gryde was followed with rapt attention. The silence was vivid. A disturbance at the door was followed by a long and angry hiss. Gryde paused. He could hear voices, one of which struck him as familiar. Somebody was trying to come in, and the doorkeeper seemed equally anxious to keep the intruder out. Then the dispute seemed to be ended and two people entered.

Not a muscle of Gryde's face moved, although in that instant he recognised the fact that he stood in the most deadly peril. To a certain extent he was prepared for this emergency—if only he were outside the hall.

But then he was penned in by thousands of people. Instantly Gryde's hand went behind him, and the touch of something hard in his pistol-pocket had a reassuring effect. For in those two men standing there grim and quiet in the door way Gryde recognised two enemies.

They were the Athens correspondent of the Chronicle and the real General Marcos!

Gryde had no occasion for any one to tell him what had happened. Either Marcos had escaped or the brigand Nicholi had betrayed him. Then these two had met, they had compared notes over fugitive English papers, and come to the logical conclusion that some one had played a daring and rascally trick upon them.

It mattered little to Gryde whom they suspected. To all practical purposes they had the daring impostor at their mercy. And meanwhile, given a few minutes' start, Gryde could have laughed at his victims. He had all his changes ready to be used the moment they were required. And in moving from town to town he had not neglected this precaution.

He spoke on quietly and steadily. Not for a fraction of a second did his iron nerve desert him. And all the time he was racking his brain for some way out. Then, with a reckless trust in his own good fortune and fertility of resource, he sat down.

By this time the enemy had pushed their way forward to the edge of the platform. The mine was about to be exploded.

"Excuse my interruption," said the "Special," with slow incisiveness, "but I have a painful task to perform. The man who has just sat down is a swindler and impostor. The gentleman by my side is the real General Marcos."

No uproar followed the statement, it was too stupendous.

"Does anybody know the speaker?" some one asked at length.

"I know him for one," the Chairman replied; "in fact, a good many of us do. This is a serious charge made by a responsible man. What does our friend say?"

The Duke turned interrogatively to Gryde. He smiled calmly.

"Nothing whatever," he responded, "only that this is a dramatic interlude which I did not anticipate. My character is entirely in your hands. If you will permit me to retire"

A burly figure on the platform barred the way.

"A, no ya don't," came the grim response. "This has to be settled here and now."

Gryde resumed his seat with a polite smile. The audience followed spellbound.

"Perhaps it would be as well," suggested the Chairman, "if those gentlemen came on the platform and made their charge in a more regular manner."

The thing was done accordingly. The "Special" was first to speak.

"What I am going to say I am in a position to prove," he said. "Who that impostor really is I neither know nor care. For the present I suspect him to be one Melville who imposed upon me under the guise of an American correspondent. The rest emanated from his own busy brain. Knowing the country well, he bribed a noted brigand, Nicholi by name, to kidnap the general. Then he proceeded to Athens with a letter of mine containing a photograph of my companion. This was artfully changed for one of his in the character he now represents. The plot was all the more ingenious because nobody in England knew the real Marcos, and so long as we saw his name in the papers we should not dream that any evil had overtaken him. Fortunately we are in time to prevent further mischief."

Gryde did not need to look up to see what effect this statement had on the audience. He could feel that they believed every word. An angry murmur swelled to a roar.

"Silence!" the Chairman cried; "we must hear the other side. Now, sir?" He turned to Gryde, who shrugged his shoulders.

"Have you nothing to say?" asked the Duke.

"Absolutely nothing," Gryde smiled. "Why fight facts?"

"Then you admit you are an impostor. If you would like to do anything—"

Gryde rose to his feet, his hand went behind him. The light of battle was in his eyes. It was one man against thousands. There was a million to one chance.

"I should like," he said, "I should like to do this."

As the last word escaped his lips he jumped from the platform to the floor. Then the gas-lights gleamed upon a revolver barrel.

"Back!" Gryde cried. "The first man who touches me dies."

The terrified crowd huddled on either side like sheep. The glare in Gryde's eyes seemed to freeze them. As one bolder than the rest put out a hand, Gryde fired past his head. Women screamed and fainted. Gryde pushed his way to the door.

His resolute will seemed to carry all before him. He could see the darkness of the street beyond. Once outside and he might yet be free. A resolute dash, and then—

Then a stalwart policeman grappled with him. A second later and others would overpower him. There was a whip-like crack, a dazzling flash, and the officer's right arm hung useless at his side. With a yell of triumph, Gryde dashed into the street.

But all danger was not yet averted. There were men young and strong in the audience who tumbled down the steps of the hall and dashed after the fugitive. Sprinting was not one of Gryde's accomplishments, and he found himself hard pressed.

More than once he doubled and turned. Folks passing stopped and wondered; and there was the chance of being pulled down at any time. Gryde became suddenly conscious that he was passing the door of his own hotel.

Could he dart sideways into this unseen and lie hidden till the foe had passed? There was just a chance that he might do so. A minute later he had flashed into the hall and taken his way up the stairs to his own room. Here he washed his face and cast off his disguise. Then he crept to the head of the stairs and listened.

Silence below, silence for a little time, and then familiar voices. Gryde could hear what they were saying distinctly. Every word he followed intently.

"We must wait till the police come," said one. "No doubt he thinks he has tricked us finely, and for the present he will remain where he is. As the fellow is armed, we shall have to proceed cautiously."

The slow minutes passed. If only Gryde had a disguise here. But that was lying hidden in a spot outside the town. A bell rang close by, a waiter came along carrying something on a tray for a sitting-room on the same landing. Gryde stood hidden in the doorway until the waiter passed again. Then he stepped out. He had made up his mind what to do.

"You are busy?" he asked.

"No, sir," responded the other, "I am just going off duty. Can I do—"

He said no more. Gryde had him by the throat with a grip like steel. He dragged the frightened man into his room and closed the door. The waiter made no struggle, he was absolutely limp with fear.

With a smile Gryde relaxed the scalding grasp.

"I should advise you not to make a noise," he suggested grimly.

"I've got a wife," the panic-stricken waiter gurgled, "and two kids, and I—"

Gryde froze the man with a look. There was no time to lose.

"Now, look here," he hissed; "if you make the slightest noise, I shall be under the painful necessity of scattering your cerebral tissue all over this very tasteful carpet. I should be sorry to do so for the sake of the landlord—and your own. If you care to listen to reason you will be the richer by £50."

The waiter showed signs of returning sanity.

"Seems to me there's no chance to do nothing else," he muttered.

"Quite so. Without asking any further questions, take off your clothes at once. Now then, see if you can do it quicker than I can."

Gryde commenced to peel off his outer garments. In an incredibly short time he had changed places with the waiter. Then he pounced upon the man and with his braces pinned him skilfully to a chair.

"The money I will put in your boot thus," he said. "I am going now, and I shall close the door behind you. See the clock yonder? When that clock ticks off five minutes you can call for help. All you have to do is to tell truthfully how you have been treated, omitting any reference to the Bank of England paper in your boot. But I don't think that I need have any anxiety on that head. You understand?"

The waiter smiled slightly. He began to see that no harm was likely to come to him from the adventure. And he was about to earn more money than he had ever had in his life before.

"All right, guvnor," he whispered hoarsely, "I'll do as you say, and I hope you'll get out of your bit of trouble all right."

Gryde smiled as he pointed to the clock.

"Once I am outside I will take care of the rest;" he said. "Five minutes, remember. I'm afraid you will have to invest in another dress suit, though."

Standing calmly before the glass, Gryde re-arranged his white tie, and then calmly left the room. Down in the hall an excited group was gathered. There were blue uniforms there amongst the rest. Gryde skirted by them without undue haste. He noted the landlord's agitated face, and heard his trembling tones.

"For heaven's sake, gentlemen," he said, "let there be no violence. It would ruin me."

"We will be careful," the Duke of Clifton was saying. "A desperate character"

Gryde waited to hear no more. The conversation was not sufficiently interesting. With a matchless audacity, all his own, he elbowed his way through the very people who were thirsting for his blood, and took his way to the hatstand. Here he selected an overcoat and hat, and putting the same on, left the hotel.

Hundreds of people had gathered there, for the news had spread like wildfire. Gryde muttered savagely to himself as he found himself shut in. At the end of five minutes he had not progressed beyond the end of the street.

Then suddenly a hoarse roar went up. It spread as if by magic to the edge of the crowd that the impostor had escaped—and how. There is no telegraphy like that which flashes through a huge concourse of people.

Gryde burst through and hailed a passing cab. He plunged in headlong.

"Get me to the top of Craven Road in ten minutes," he shouted, "and I'll give you a sovereign."

The driver whipped up his horse, and was in a deserted side street immediately, neither was he aware of the nature of his fare. In the given time the destination was reached.

Gryde paid his man, and hurried away into the darkness. There was a wild thrill of triumph at his heart, for he was free. He was close to the place where his disguise was hidden, and before midnight the same was assumed, and the dress clothes sunk at the bottom of a deep pool. By daybreak a respectable looking mechanic passed out of Nottingham station to the other side of the town.

Later in the afternoon, Gryde, in propria persona, travelled up to London in a first-class carriage.

"This is the last time," he told himself. "I have more money than anyone wants, and sooner or later I'm certain to make some mistake. I'll destroy all my wardrobe and settle down as a model country gentleman."

In one of the most perfectly appointed houses in the North lives Felix Gryde, an English-American, who is reputed to have made a fabulous fortune in the States. Gryde is a popular and respected figure, and his popularity is shared by a wife who is called Cora. Mrs. Gryde takes a prominent place in society, and the younger men find her extremely fascinating. Like most women, she imagines that her husband has no secrets from her, in which she is greatly mistaken—Gryde's adventures will never be told by him.

"If I had my deserts," he frequently tells himself, "I should be a life convict. And after all there are thousands of greater scoundrels ruling the country and helping to make our laws. They have not been found out, neither have I. And assuredly the wicked flourish like a green bay tree. I ought to know"

FRED M WHITE – A CONCISE BIBLIOGRAPHY

NOVELS (A-Z)

Ambition's Slave (1916)
The Argus Eye (1919)
Blackmail (1902)
The Blue Daffodil (1934)
The Brand Of Silence (1911)
A Broken Memory (1929)
The Bubble Reputation (1908)
By Order Of The League (1886)
The Cardinal Moth aka The Accused Orchid (1903)
The Case For the Crown (1918)
Claxton's Mill (1912)
A Clue In Wax (1930)
The Corner House (1905)
The Councillors of Falconhoe (1922)
Craven Fortune (1904)
A Crime On Canvas (1909)
The Crimson Blind (US title: The Mystery Of The Crimson Blind) (1905)
A Daughter Of Israel (1892)
The Day: Or The Passing Of A Throne (1914)
A Deal In Letters (1923)
The Devil's Advocate (1924)
Dropped From The Fast Express, or A Daughter's Sacrifice (1911)
The Edge Of The Sword (1907)
The Ends Of Justice (1906)
A Fatal Dose (aka Behind the Mask) (1907)
The Fight For The Child (1925)
The Five Knots (1907)
"Found Dead" (1930)
The Four Fingers (US title: The Mystery Of The Four Fingers) (1907)
A Front Of Brass (1910)
The Garden O' Dreams (1909)
A Golden Argosy (1886)
The Golden Bat (1924)
The Golden Rose (1909)
The Green Bungalow (1923)
The Grey Woman (aka Sinister House) (1928)

The Happy Exile (1920)
A Harbour Of Refuge (1918)
Hard Pressed (1910)
The Honour Of His House (1920)
The House Of Mammon (1913)
A House Of Sorrows (1911)
The House Of The Schemers (1906)
The House On The River (1925)
In Trust (1892)
Jim Crowshaw's Mary (1911)
The King Diamond (1927)
Lady Clara (1913)
Lady Edna's Awakening (1920)
The Lady In Blue (1915)
The Law Of The Land (1906)
The Leopard's Spots (1920)
The Lonely Bride (aka The White Bride) (1907)
The Lord Of The Manor (1907)
Love, The Foe (1910)
A Maker of Millions (1909)
The Man Called Gilray (1911)
The Man Who Found Christmas (a novelette) (1915)
The Man Who Knew (1932)
The Man Who Was Two (1921)
The Man With The Vandyk Beard (1925)
The Midnight Guest: A Detective Story (1907)
A Mummer's Throne (1910)
My Lady Bountiful (1905)
The Mystery Of Crocksands (1923)
The Mystery Of The Ravenspurs (aka The Black Valley) (1911)
The Mystery Of Room 75 (1922)
Naboth's Vineyard (1889)
The Nether Millstone (1906)
Netta, The Story Of Sin (1909)
New Century Calendar Clue (1948)
Number Thirteen (1914)
The Old Secretaire: A Christmas Story (novelette) (1887)
On The Night Express (1930)
The Open Door (1907)
Paul Quentin (1908)
Paul, The Sage (1910)
The Phantom Car (1929)
Powers Of Darkness (1912)
The Price Of Silence (1925)
The Psalm Stone (1905)
Queen Of Hearts (1930)
A Queen Of The Stage (1908)
The Riddle Of The Rail (1926)

The Robe Of Lucifer (1896)
A Royal Wrong (1913)
The Salt Of The Earth (1918)
The Scales Of Justice (1908)
Secret Of The River (1934)
The Secret Of The Sands (1911)
A Secret Service (1913)
The Seed Of Empire (1916)
The Sentence Of The Court (1913)
A Shadowed Love (1905)
The Shadow Of The Dead Hand (1926)
The Silver Stream (novelette)
The Slave Of Silence (1906)
A Society Jezebel (1917)
The Sundial (1908)
Tregarthen's Wife: A Cornish Story (1901)
The Turn Of The Tide (1923)
The Weight Of The Crown (1904)
The White Battalions (1900)
The White Bride (aka The Lonely Bride) (1910)
The White Glove (1910)
The Wings Of Victory (1919)
The Yellow Face (1906)

SHORT FICTION SERIES

THE MASTER CRIMINAL (1897-1898)

A series of 12 short stories featuring Felix Gryde, who describes himself as "a really clever soldier of fortune."

The Head Of The Caesars
At Windsor
The Silverpool Cup
The "Morrison Raid" Indemnity
Cleopatra's Robe
The Rosy Cross
The Death Of The President
The Cradlestone Oil Mills
Redburn Castle
"Crysoline Limited"
The Loss Of The "Eastern Empress"
General Marcos

THE LAST OF THE BORGIAS (1898)

A series of stories featuring Professor Victor Colonna, a vigilante physician who murders undesirable people with undetectable poisons.

The Scrip of Death
The Crimson Streak
The Holy Rose
The Saving Of Serena
The Varteg Necklace
The Three Carnations

DRENTON DENN - SPECIAL COMMISSIONER

Drenton Denn is a tough newspaper reporter on the payroll of The New York Post. His hallmarks are a straw hat, a Norfolk jacket, a perennial cigar, and a terrier by the name of "Prince."

The Yellow Moth
The Red Speck
Dust
The Fire Bugs
The Great White Moth

THE ROMANCE OF THE SECRET SERVICE FUND (1900)

This series features Newton Moore, the top agent at The Secret Service Fund.

By Woman's Wit
The Mazaroff Rifle
In The Express
The Almedi Concession
The Other Side Of The Chess Board
Three Of Them

THE DOOM OF LONDON

This sci-fi series of six stories describes a variety of catastrophes which ravage London.

The Four White Days
The Four Days' Night
The Dust Of Death
A Bubble Burst
The Invisible Force
The River Of Death

THE SAGE OF TYBURN (1905-1906)

Each of these stories was preceded by the header The Sage Of Tyburn.

No. 1 - The Chronicle Of The Yellow Girl
No. 2 - The Chronicle Of The Blue-Eyed Syndicate
No. 3 - The Chronicle Of The Inconsequent Princess
No. 4 - The Chronicle Of The Elderly Adonis
No. 5 - The Chronicle Of The Libelled Velasquez

THE DRAGON-FLY (1909)

Six stories about an impecunious but brilliant amateur criminologist, entomologist and ornithologist by the name of Horace Daimler. Each of the stories was preceded by the header The Dragon-Fly.

No. 1 - How Horace Daimler Got His Name
No. 2 - The Three Red Rats
No. 3 - [title unknown]
No. 4 - [title unknown]
No. 5 - A [illegible] Crime
No. 6 - The Mirror Over The Fireplace

REAL DRAMA (1909)

A series of stories published under the subtitle "Being Some Leaves From The Notebook Of A Late Theatrical Agent."

His Second Self
An Extra Turn
"Not In The Bill"
The Plagiarist
The Man In Possession
A Pair Of Handcuffs

THE TELEPHONE STAR (1912)

A series of stories about Keith Marrit, a star journalist working for a fictitious newspaper called The Telephone.

No. 1 - The Case Of El Hamid, The Seer
No. 2 - The Case Of The Genuine Counterfeit
No. 3 - The Case Of The Yellow Car
No. 4 - The Case Of Lord Wintercotte
No. 5 - The Case Of The Rusty Nail
No. 6 - The Case Of The One-Eyed Chauffeur

The Barrister At Bay
Below Zero
The Better Way
Big Fish
The Big Thing
Billy's Xmas
A Bit Of Egypt
The Black Admiral
The Black Cat
The Black Narcissus
The Black Prince
Blind
Blind Chance
The Blindworm
A Block Of Marble
A Bootless Errand
Brayton's Secret
The Broken Lute
A Broken Sceptre
The Broken Trail
The Buff Gauntlet
Burglar Bill's Pupil
By Grace Of His Majesty
By Wireless
A Call On The Phone
A Captious Critic
The Case For The Prisoner
The Charlatan
A Christmas Bride
A Christmas Deputy
Christmas Cards
The Christmas Carol
A Christmas in Peril
A Christmas Star
The Clock Struck Twelve
The Colonel's Christmas Pudding
Compounding A Felony
The Convict
Coralie And The Pearls
A Corner In Elephants
The Courage Of Despair
Crossed Swords
The Dancing Shadow
The Daughters Of The Moon
A Daughter Of Nature
The Dawnstar
A Deal In Diamonds
Denny

A Derelict In Clover
The Desert Ship
A Dog's Life
The Doll's House
The Dormer Window
A Dose Of Quinine
The Doubting D, or, A Cranky Cryptogram
A Draught Of Life
Early Closing Day
An Eastern Princess
The Eavesdropper
The Ebbing Tide
The Egg Of The Little Auk
The Emsdam Dispatches
The Empty House
An Error Of Judgment
The Evidence For The Prisoner
Excess Profits
An Eye For An Eye
The Eye Of The Camera
The First Stone
The Foil
Forget-Me-Not
For Love's Sake
For Once In A Way
For Value Received
A Foster-Father
Found!
The Fourth Man
Free Labour
A Friendly Call
From Information Received
Full Fathoms Deep
Gabrielle
A Gamble In Love
A Game Of Draughts
A Garden Of Pearls
Gentlemen Of The Jury
The Gates Of Ramshi
The Grey Bat
The Grey Raider
The Guiding Star
The Half-Crown Princess
The Hand Invisible
Hardy's Big Coup
The Heart Of The Anarchist
Heavy Metal
The Heels Of The Dawn

Her Christmas Dawn
His Christmas Gift
His Majesty's Mails
A Hole In The Net
The Hospitallers
Ice In June: A Playwright's Story
Icky Of Oluk Lake
Imperial Preference
In Black And White
In Rosemary Lane
In The Dark
In The Fog
In The Pit
Introducing Mr. Pentsymon
The Joinville Tunnel
Judgment Reserved
Karma
Kindergarten
The Kingmaker's Token
Lady Mary's Bulldog
The Language Of Flowers
The Last Drive
The Law Of The Jungle: A Tale Of Mean Streets
The Leather-Pushin' Private
The Left Hand
The Lesson The Ants Taught
The Livery Of Death
The Lonely Furrow
The Long Arm Of Bronze
Love In Aether
The Luck Of The Game
Made In England
The Man Himself
The Man Who Got Through
The Man Who Rang The Bell
The Man With The Eyeglass
A Masked Battery
The Master's Voice
A Matter Of Habit
'Merica
A Message from the Flood
The Midnight Call
The Missing Blade
The Missing Note
The Mistletoe Bough
Moray The Traitor
More Than Coronets
The Morning Glory

Music Hath Charms
A Musical Treat
The Mystery Of Room Five
Natural Selection
Nerves
The Night Express: The Story Of A Bank Robbery
The Northern Light
Not On The Records
An Object Lesson
The Odds On Zero
One Day With A Working Ant
One Foggy Night
One Of The Old Guard
On Peace Night
The Onus Of The Charge
The Orpheusia
Ostentation
The Other Man's Story
The Pardon
A Parrot Cry
The Path Of Progress
The Pawn And The Rook
Pearls Of Price
Photo By Lesterre
Pictures In The Snow (a Christmas story)
A Place In The Sun
The Platinum Chain
A Popular Novelist
Poste Restante
A Prize Crop
Proof Positive
The Purple Terror
A Queen In Hiding
A Question Of Money
Rachel's Seventh Year
Rawhide Science
The Real Dramatic Touch
A Record Round
Red Petals
Rob Peter—Pay Paul
A Rope Of Snow
Rose Of The Desert
A Royal Bag
The Royal Train
The Salmon Poachers
Santa Anna
A Satisfactory Reference
Saviour From The North

The Second Chapter
Second In The Field
The Shebeeners
A Single Hair
Sir Jeremiah's Big Shoot
Sister Louise
The Sixteenth Chapter
A Sleeping Partner
Sleeping Partner
A Sound In The Night
"Special" To The Telephone
A Stolen Interview
The Straight Game
The Stranger Within The Gate
Sub Rosa
The Substitute
The Superman
The Supreme Test
The Sword Of Justice
A Table Tragedy
The Thirty-Seventh Month
This Little World
A Thrilling Exit
The Throat Of The Wolf
The Ticket
To Be Let Furnished
Treasures Three
The Two Bon-Bons
Two Of Them
The Unbelieving Eye
Unbidden Guests
The Unexpected
An Unrecorded Crime
The Vital Spark
The Vital Spot
War Ribbons
The Waterwitch
The Western Way
When The Moon Set
The White Geranium
The White Spot
White Wings (1922)
The Wings Of Chance (1922)
The Witness (1920)
The World Next Door (1916)